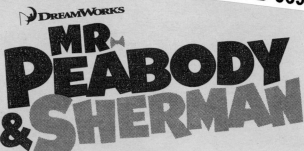

The Junior Novelization

Published in the United States by Random House,
a division of Random House LLC, 1745 Broadway, New York, NY 10019, and
in Canada by Random House of Canada Limited, Toronto, Penguin Random
House Companies. Random House and the colophon
are registered trademarks of Random House LLC.
randomhouse.com/kids
ISBN 978-0-385-37141-4
Printed in the United States of America
10 9 8 7 6 5 4 3 2 1

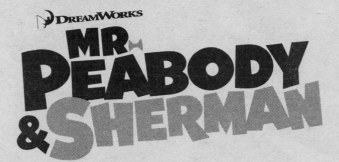

The Junior Novelization

Adapted by Erica David

Random House New York

Prologue

Dear Reader,

    Allow me to introduce myself. Peabody here. You may have heard of some of my accomplishments. I'm a scientist, an inventor, a Nobel Prize winner, and an Olympic gold medalist, but my greatest achievement is being father to my adopted son, Sherman. When people see us together, they're often surprised. After all, it's not every day that a literate dog such as myself wins the right to raise a human boy.

    When it comes to being a good parent, I leave nothing to chance, especially when it comes to my boy's education. So I did what any father would do: I invented a time machine. That way Sherman could see history firsthand.

    What follows is our story. It's the simple tale of a dog and his boy, their time machine, and what happens when the universe tries to pull them apart. It's one adventure Sherman and I will never forget!

Sincerely,
Mr. Peabody, PhD, Esq., DOG, etc., etc.

"What should I do, Mr. Peabody?" Sherman asked. The boy's eyes were wide with fear. He stood in front of a mob of angry French peasants who pushed and stomped and waved their torches in the air.

"Off with his head!" the mob shouted.

Sherman winced. His father, the brilliant scientist and inventor Mr. Peabody, had been clapped into a guillotine in the middle of a public square. A sharp blade hung suspended above his neck. Within seconds the executioner would drop the blade and chop off his head with a **thwack**!

"Mr. Peabody, what should I do?" he asked again nervously.

"Nothing, Sherman!" Mr. Peabody replied. There was

no reason for his son to worry. As usual, Mr. Peabody had it all figured out.

✺

Mr. Peabody and Sherman had gotten into the sticky situation earlier that day, when they had attended a party. But not just any party . . .

Mr. Peabody led Sherman into a grand ballroom in the luxurious palace of Marie Antoinette, the queen of France. The party was taking place in the year 1789—more than two hundred years in the past! Fortunately, time travel was no obstacle for Mr. Peabody. He'd built a time machine called the WABAC (pronounced "way back"). It allowed him to travel to famous moments in history—such as the French Revolution—and teach Sherman all about them.

Sherman blinked in wonder behind his thick glasses. He'd never seen so many fancy foods and fancy people in one place. French aristocrats were dressed in expensive silk clothing with bows that made them look like neatly wrapped presents. The queen's dress was so ornate and colorful, she looked like a fancy dessert. She was a pudgy, round woman whose fluffy white hair was piled high on her head like a tower of whipped cream.

Mr. Peabody introduced Sherman to the queen.

Sherman was delighted to meet her, but he was even more delighted to see the enormous cake on the table next to her. It was taller than him, and absolutely smothered in frosting.

"Wow! That's a lot of cake, Mr. Peabody," Sherman said.

"Marie Antoinette was a woman with a prodigious appetite for all things . . . covered with frosting. But her expensive tastes made her the target of much criticism," Mr. Peabody explained.

"Why?" Sherman asked.

"Because during Marie's reign, the common people of France were exceedingly poor," answered Mr. Peabody.

Sherman nodded. He tried to understand what his father was telling him, but when he looked at the cake again, his stomach rumbled in anticipation. "Can I have some cake now?" he asked the queen.

"Mais oui," Marie replied.

"Sorry," he said. **"MAY WE** have some cake?"

"MAIS OUI," the queen answered.

Confused, Sherman turned to Mr. Peabody. "Can she not hear me through the hair?"

Mr. Peabody started to explain that *mais oui* means "of course," but the queen shouted, **"LET ZEM EAT CAKE!"**

The queen's voice rang through the palace. Through a window, two French peasants in the courtyard were spying on her party. When they heard what she'd said, they got angry. Why should she and her fancy friends have cake when they were poor and starving? The spies raced away to tell the other peasants what they had heard.

Soon a huge mob of angry peasants carrying torches gathered outside the palace. They were determined to storm the castle and round up the wealthy aristocrats. The peasants shouted, stomped their feet, and threw rocks at the palace windows.

"Vive la Révolution!" they yelled.

Suddenly, a large brick smashed through the ballroom window and landed in Marie's cake. Mr. Peabody realized it was time to leave. He said goodbye to the queen and turned to go but discovered Sherman was missing.

"Sherman? Sherman!" he called, looking frantically around the room.

Just then, the ballroom doors burst open and the mob of peasants barged in. They took one look at Mr. Peabody in his fancy clothes and narrowed their eyes. They thought he was one of the rich aristocrats.

"Seize him!" they roared.

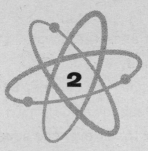

2

The angry peasants dragged Mr. Peabody to the public square and clapped him into the guillotine. Sherman was scared. He watched as the peasants' leader, Robespierre, addressed the crowd.

"The queen and her aristocratic cronies must pay the price for their gluttony! We will slaughter them like the dogs that they are—starting with this one!" Robespierre yelled. He pointed to Mr. Peabody, whose head was trapped in the guillotine's wooden stock.

A black-hooded executioner prepared to drop the blade. Sherman rocked anxiously on his feet. "Mr. Peabody, what should I do?" he asked.

"Nothing, Sherman!" Mr. Peabody answered. His eyes darted from the executioner to Sherman's glasses to a sewer lid just a few feet away.

"But, Mr. Peabody—"

"Everything's going to be fine, Sherman; just stay right there!" Mr. Peabody said firmly.

The sun began to set over the square. Suddenly, its bright rays slanted through the air and struck the corner of Sherman's glasses. He was momentarily blinded by the shining light, but he still heard the awful sound of the guillotine's blade as it dropped. **Thunk!**

"Mr. Peabody!" Sherman wailed.

Robespierre reached into the basket in front of the guillotine and pulled out Mr. Peabody's head—only it wasn't a head at all. It was half of a melon!

Robespierre smashed the melon and pounded his foot on the ground in rage. He'd been tricked. He quickly spun around, looking for any sign of Mr. Peabody. He turned just in time to see him grab Sherman and disappear down the hole beneath the sewer lid.

"Get that dog!" Robespierre screamed.

Mr. Peabody and Sherman landed in the sewers with a **splash!** As they ran through the dark, twisting tunnels, Sherman asked, "Mr. Peabody, how'd you escape?"

"Simple, really. I noticed the distance between the sewer lids, noted the loose board under the basket, computed the angle at which the setting sun would bounce off your glasses, momentarily blinding the executioner, and chose that moment to swipe the executioner's melon, giving me the added weight to tip the boards, facilitating my exit," Mr. Peabody answered.

"That's amazing," Sherman said, impressed.

"It's not amazing. It was just a matter of keeping my head." Mr. Peabody winked.

"Ha! Keeping your head!" Sherman snorted. Then his eyebrows drew together in a puzzled frown. "I don't get it."

Mr. Peabody had no time to explain the details of his clever pun. A sewer lid rumbled, and a shaft of light spilled into the manhole. Robespierre and his peasant guards dropped into the tunnel, landing right in front of them.

"There he is! After them!" Robespierre called out.

Mr. Peabody and Sherman made a sharp turn and dove quickly into a side tunnel. They raced along the dark passages, listening carefully for any sign of Robespierre and his guards. They turned left, then right, then left again. Sherman was beginning to think they were running in circles. Finally, they rounded a corner and came face to face with Robespierre.

"Aha! I got you now!" the Frenchman said triumphantly, pulling out his sword. Mr. Peabody cast a quick glance over his shoulder to see a group of guards approaching from behind. It looked like Robespierre was right. They were trapped!

Mr. Peabody remained calm. There was no situation he couldn't think his way out of. He just needed a moment to come up with a plan. "What a master of the chase you are, Monsieur Robespierre," he said, stalling for time.

"Oh, you noticed?" Robespierre asked proudly.

"Of course! Doubling back on me like that—that was genius!" Mr. Peabody told him. He glanced up and down the tunnel, noting the number of guards, the distance between the sewer lids, and the peculiar odor wafting through the smelly corridor. His eyes lit up as a particularly clever idea occurred to him.

"I just hope you don't take my little confederate here." Mr. Peabody nodded at Sherman. "I depend on him so completely."

Robespierre dashed forward and yanked Sherman to his side, pointing his sword directly at Mr. Peabody's nose.

"Drat! You're devilishly clever!" said Mr. Peabody.

"I know, and much quicker than you as well," Robespierre said smugly.

"But are you quick enough for this?" In the blink of an eye, Mr. Peabody tossed the other half of the executioner's melon at Robespierre. Without thinking, Robespierre caught the melon and dropped his sword, which Mr. Peabody deftly plucked from the air.

"Aha! See? Quick!" said Robespierre before he realized what had happened.

"Quick, yes, but not too smart!" Mr. Peabody responded. He waved the sword in front of his opponent's eyes.

Robespierre scowled. He tossed the melon away, snatched a sword from one of his guards, and moved in for the attack. His blade whistled through the air and struck Mr. Peabody's sword with a resounding clang.

"All right, Sherman—looks like it's time for a little pop quiz in the art of fencing!" Mr. Peabody announced.

"Attack! Parry! Thrust!" Sherman called. Mr. Peabody advanced with swift, nimble steps, executing each of Sherman's commands. The blade of his sword slashed back and forth so quickly, it was almost a blur.

Robespierre lunged with his sword aimed directly

at Mr. Peabody's head. But Mr. Peabody was too fast for him. He ducked and slid through Robespierre's legs, popping up right behind him. He continued his attack, backing Robespierre down the tunnel until the Frenchman stood directly beneath a sewer lid.

In two swift strides, Mr. Peabody rushed Robespierre and knocked the sword from his hand. The sword flew into the air, spinning end over end, and hit the sewer lid overhead. The lid rattled, flipped, and dropped straight down, landing directly on Robespierre's head. The Frenchman collapsed in an unconscious heap.

The guards gasped as their leader keeled over. But they had little time to recover before Mr. Peabody threw his sword at them. They ducked quickly, and the sword lodged in the sewer wall behind them.

"Ha, ha! You missed!" the guards taunted.

Mr. Peabody flashed a dashing grin. "I never miss."

The sewer wall trembled and burst, filling the tunnel with water.

"Oh, non! Sacre bleu!" the guards cried as the wave engulfed them.

Mr. Peabody grabbed Sherman and jumped onto the sewer lid that had struck Robespierre. As the water roared into the tunnel, the lid began to float, carrying the two of them on the surface of the wave. Holding tight to the lid, they surfed along the passage toward the exit.

"Do you smell that, Sherman?" Mr. Peabody asked, wrinkling his nose.

"It wasn't me, Mr. Peabody," Sherman answered innocently.

"I know it wasn't you. It's the methane gas in the sewer system, and given the fact that it ignites at three hundred and six degrees Fahrenheit, we're about to use it to blast out of here!" Mr. Peabody explained.

He leaned on the metal edge of the sewer lid and scraped it against a tunnel wall, causing sparks to appear. The sparks ignited the gas in the tunnel, and— **ka-BOOM!**—created a huge explosion, which blasted Mr. Peabody and Sherman out of the sewer.

The force of the blast sent them sailing over the glittering city. The erupting gas lit up the Paris sky like fireworks.

"Whoo-hoo!" Sherman cheered as they sailed through the fiery night. Mr. Peabody brought them in for a smooth landing, using the sewer lid like a skateboard to ride down the side of a tree in the forest outside the palace of Versailles. Unharmed, they dusted themselves off and walked toward where Mr. Peabody had parked the WABAC.

"So, what did you learn today, Sherman?" asked Mr. Peabody.

"The French Revolution was crazy!" Sherman replied. "All those guys getting their heads chopped off and nobody standing up and saying it wasn't right!"

"And to think, Marie Antoinette could have avoided the whole revolution if she'd simply issued an edict to distribute bread amongst the poor," said Mr. Peabody.

Sherman nodded. He knew "edict" was just a fancy word for "law."

"But then she couldn't have had her dessert," Mr. Peabody said.

"Why not?" Sherman asked.

"Because, Sherman, you can't have your cake and *edict*, too," Mr. Peabody said, chuckling.

Sherman laughed at Mr. Peabody's joke, but then his brows drew together in confusion.

"I don't get it," he said, puzzled.

Mr. Peabody simply smiled and turned to the empty clearing in front of them. At first glance, there was nothing but grass and trees, but suddenly, the WABAC materialized, its reflective tiles flipping over as Mr.

Peabody and Sherman approached. The camouflaged time machine was quickly revealed in all its glory. It was a red sphere with a shiny metallic finish that glinted in the moonlight. The WABAC hovered above the ground, defying gravity and humming with energy.

Together father and son climbed aboard the ship and settled into their chairs in front of the futuristic navigation console. Sherman was ready for another journey through history, but Mr. Peabody set a course for home. Sherman's jaw dropped open in surprise when Mr. Peabody reminded him that, in fact, he *was* about to go on a different kind of adventure: "Tomorrow is your first day of school!"

3

Early the next morning, Mr. Peabody brought his motorcycle to a stop outside Susan B. Anthony Elementary School. Sherman hopped excitedly from the sidecar and pulled off his helmet and goggles. He couldn't wait for his first day of school to begin.

Mr. Peabody had been giving him advice all morning, and now that they had finally arrived, Sherman was more than ready to head off on his own. But before he could race inside, Mr. Peabody gave him a special present. It was a shiny silver dog whistle.

Sherman blew hard into the whistle and was disappointed when no sound came out. "It doesn't work, Mr. Peabody," he said, looking at it inquisitively.

Mr. Peabody had clamped his paws over his sensitive ears. "It works, Sherman. It's just a frequency only dogs can hear," he explained patiently.

Sherman nodded and slipped the whistle into his back pocket, eager to get to class.

"Let that little keepsake be a reminder to you that no matter what challenges you may face," Mr. Peabody began, "no matter how far away I might seem—"

"Bye, Mr. Peabody!" Sherman cut him off. He waved briefly, ran up the front steps, and disappeared inside the school.

". . . I'm with you." Mr. Peabody heaved a lonely sigh. School was one adventure that he would have to let Sherman face on his own.

Sherman's first day of school started with a history lesson about George Washington. History was Sherman's specialty. Thanks to the WABAC, he knew all about the past.

"Who can tell me who George Washington was?" the teacher asked.

"Oh, me! I can, I can!" Sherman answered eagerly. His hand shot into the air. He didn't notice the equally eager blond girl sitting at the desk just behind him. Her hand was poised in the air, and she stared hard at the teacher, vying for attention.

When the teacher called on Sherman, the girl narrowed her eyes at him.

"George Washington was the first president of the United States," Sherman answered.

The teacher nodded and asked her next question. "And when President Washington was a little boy, what kind of tree did he cut down?"

Again, Sherman raised his hand excitedly, but the blond girl was equally determined.

The teacher called on her. "Penny?"

"A cherry tree!" Penny replied.

"Apocryphal!" Sherman exclaimed.

The class gasped at the rude-sounding word, but Sherman assured them that it was just a fancy way of saying "false."

"George Washington never cut down a cherry tree, and he never said he couldn't lie. People made those stories up to teach kids a lesson about lying, but they're not true," Sherman explained. "But Washington *did* cross the Delaware River on Christmas night in 1776. My dad took me there over the summer!"

The teacher smiled, impressed with Sherman's knowledge. "Well, it looks like someone really knows their history, huh, Penny?" she said.

Penny frowned and folded her arms across her chest. She wasn't about to let Sherman upstage her. She would have to show this kid who was boss.

Sherman was having lunch in the cafeteria with his new friends, Mason and Carl, when Penny and her friends walked up to him.

"Whaddaya got there, Sherman? Kibbles or bits?" Penny asked with a fake smile.

"Actually, I've got baby carrots, organic apple juice, and a tuna sandwich," Sherman said. "It's super-high in omega-threes."

"So you eat human food, huh?" Penny sneered.

"Yeah, why wouldn't I?" asked Sherman.

"Because *you* are a dog," Penny taunted him.

"No, I'm not," Sherman said stiffly.

"Sure, you are. Your dad's a dog, so you are, too." Penny smirked. "Here, I'll show you."

She snatched Sherman's sandwich from his lunch tray and tossed it across the room. "Fetch!"

Sherman didn't know what to do.

"Go on, doggy, go get your lunch! **Ruff, ruff!**" Penny barked.

The kids in the cafeteria started laughing. Sherman's

friends tried to stick up for him, but Penny told them to mind their own business. Finally, Sherman stood and went to get his sandwich, hoping Penny would leave him alone. But as soon as he walked past her, she reached into his pocket and grabbed his dog whistle.

"What's this?" she asked scornfully.

"It's mine. Give it back," Sherman said through clenched teeth. He was trying to put up with Penny, but now she was making him mad. He lunged for the whistle. Penny twirled away from him and held the whistle high above her head.

"Jump, doggy, jump!" she goaded him.

Furious, Sherman leapt for the whistle, but Penny was ready for him. She grabbed him around the neck and pulled him into a headlock.

Sherman twisted and tried to break free. "Let me go!" he growled.

"Not until you beg like a dog!" Penny said nastily. "Come on, Sherman, beg!"

That was the final straw. Sherman wasn't about to beg. He elbowed Penny and wrestled her to the ground. Then he snarled and really let her have it.

4

To Principal Purdy's surprise, Mr. Peabody was the happiest parent ever to be called into the principal's office at Susan B. Anthony Elementary School.

"I fully expected this," Mr. Peabody said, smiling, "and as with all things Sherman-related, I prepared for it!"

"You did?" Principal Purdy asked timidly. Most parents dreaded a visit to his office.

Mr. Peabody nodded enthusiastically. He popped open his briefcase and pulled out a folder containing a special curriculum just for Sherman. As the son of a Nobel Prize–winning scientist, the boy would of course be ready for advanced work. *Like father, like son,* he thought.

Principal Purdy shook his head. He hadn't called

Mr. Peabody in to discuss Sherman's academic achievements. "Sherman got into a fight today, in the lunchroom . . . with a girl," he explained.

Mr. Peabody froze. The smile faded from his face. "Oh dear," he gasped.

"Pictures were taken for insurance purposes," Principal Purdy told him nervously. He showed several pictures to Mr. Peabody. They weren't pretty. The last of them showed a huge bite mark on Penny's arm.

"He *bit* her," said an unfamiliar voice.

Mr. Peabody turned in his chair to see a large, imposing woman in a dark gray suit. She had stern features and a commanding presence as she scowled down at him.

"I am Miss Grunion from the Bureau of Child Safety and Protection," she said. "Principal Purdy notified me about the situation regarding your adopted son, Sherman. I have a few standard questions." Miss Grunion pulled out a clipboard and pencil and fixed Mr. Peabody with a hard stare. "Is the boy running roughshod over you back at the house?"

"No," Mr. Peabody answered.

"Chewing on things?" she asked.

"No," Mr. Peabody replied, offended. "Just what are you getting at?"

"In my opinion, a dog can never be a suitable parent to a little boy," Miss Grunion said, sneering.

Mr. Peabody straightened in his chair. He was shocked. He'd worked so hard to be a good father. "I must point out, Miss Grunion, that I won the right to adopt Sherman in a court of law," he said.

"And the court can take it away from you," Miss Grunion said, her voice full of menace as she glared at him. "I'll be coming to your home tomorrow evening to conduct an investigation. If I discover that you are in any way an unfit parent, I will see to it that Sherman is removed from your custody. *Permanently.* Do I make myself clear?"

"Crystal." Mr. Peabody gulped. Miss Grunion was a formidable opponent . . . and the stakes were high.

In the Manhattan penthouse that Mr. Peabody and Sherman called home, it was time for bed. After brushing his teeth and putting on his pajamas, Sherman apologized for biting Penny.

"That kind of wanton violence is totally

unacceptable," Mr. Peabody scolded Sherman, tucking him into bed. "And uncharacteristic, given how you feel about Mr. Gandhi. What on earth provoked it?"

"She called me a dog," Sherman muttered, embarrassed.

Mr. Peabody's ears drooped. If there was one thing he hadn't prepared for in all his research, it was how Sherman might feel about having a dog for a dad.

For once in his life, Mr. Peabody didn't know what to say. "Well, all right, then," he mumbled uncomfortably. "Try to get some sleep."

He switched off the light in Sherman's bedroom and walked toward the door.

"I love you, Mr. Peabody," Sherman called.

Mr. Peabody stopped and looked at him. There was so much he wanted to say, but he found that he could only reply stiffly, "I have a deep regard for you as well, Sherman."

Then he quickly shut the door, leaving Sherman in the dark.

Later that night, Mr. Peabody paced anxiously. The situation with Miss Grunion was serious, and he was worried. If she proved he was an unfit parent, he could lose Sherman forever! The idea was unthinkable.

Mr. Peabody remembered all the wonderful times he'd had with Sherman since he adopted him as a baby. Sherman's first steps. Sherman's first words. Sherman's first trip in the WABAC. He wasn't about to give the boy up without a fight.

Mr. Peabody scratched his chin in thought. After all, there was no situation he couldn't think his way out of. His brow furrowed in concentration. Moments later, he had a brilliant idea!

It was the perfect plan.

5

The following evening, Sherman found Mr. Peabody bustling around the kitchen. He was busy cooking. Shiny silver pots full of delicious soups and sauces crowded the stove, and platter after platter of gourmet food covered the countertops.

"Wow! Is today some kind of special occasion?" Sherman asked.

"You could say that," Mr. Peabody answered mysteriously.

Just then, the doorbell rang. Mr. Peabody pulled off his apron and chef's hat and went to answer the door. Sherman followed, curious to see who was coming to dinner. He was shocked—a little freaked out, actually—when the door opened to reveal Penny and her parents, Paul and Patty Peterson.

"Welcome," Mr. Peabody said, flashing the Petersons a charming smile.

Paul Peterson's eyes widened in surprise. "So he's *literally* a dog?" he asked his wife.

"Paul!" Patty shushed him.

"No, that's all right. Although, I prefer 'literate dog,'" Mr. Peabody replied graciously.

Patty Peterson chuckled, but Paul remained unimpressed. He looked at Mr. Peabody suspiciously.

"Say hello to Penny, Sherman," Mr. Peabody prompted.

Sherman forced a smile and said hello. Penny was pretty much the last person he wanted to see. From the expression on her face, it was clear she felt the same way.

"Now why don't you go show Penny your mineral collection, Sherman?" Mr. Peabody suggested. "I'm sure she'll find those new geodes of yours fascinating."

Reluctantly, Sherman took Penny off to his room, but not before he gave Mr. Peabody a wounded look.

Mr. Peabody led the Petersons into the living room. "I'm so glad you accepted my invitation. Now the kids can resolve their differences in a more civilized manner," he said brightly. Mr. Peabody knew that smoothing things over with Penny's parents would be a good way to prevent Miss Grunion from taking Sherman away.

"I'm not here to be civilized," Paul grumbled. "In fact, if it weren't for Patty, I would have pressed charges already. And I have to tell you, Peabody, where my daughter is concerned, nothing is more important than her safety!"

Mr. Peabody sighed. Becoming friends with the Petersons wasn't going to be as easy as he'd thought.

In Sherman's room, Sherman and Penny spent most of the evening ignoring each other. The one time he tried to talk to her, she hissed, "If you say one word to me, jerkface, I'll **hurt** you."

That was enough to convince Sherman to keep his distance. He could have easily ignored her all night if Mr. Peabody hadn't popped in to check on them. He pulled Sherman aside and encouraged him to make friends with Penny.

"Share your interests. Tell her a witty anecdote," he advised.

Mr. Peabody made it sound so easy. He had no idea what Sherman was dealing with.

After Mr. Peabody had returned to his guests,

Sherman glanced at Penny. She was sitting on the opposite side of the room playing a video game on her phone. A few minutes later, Sherman worked up the courage to speak to her.

"You know, Penny, Sigmund Freud says if you don't like a person, it's because they remind you of something you don't like about yourself," he said.

Penny rolled her eyes. "What do you know about Sigmund Freud?" she asked skeptically.

"More than you think," Sherman replied.

Penny jumped to her feet. "Sure. Just like you know all that stuff about George Washington not cutting down the cherry tree," she sneered. "What a crock."

"But it's true!" Sherman protested.

"How do you know?" Penny pressed.

"I just know!" Sherman shouted. He wasn't telling the whole truth, but he didn't have a choice. Mr. Peabody always warned him not to tell anyone about the WABAC.

Penny propped her hands on her hips and took a slow step toward Sherman. He backed away nervously.

"Did you read it in a book?" she asked menacingly.

Sherman shook his head. Penny asked question after question, marching Sherman across the room, until at last his back was against the wall.

Fed up, Penny poked a threatening finger into his chest. "So how do you know, Sherman?" she demanded.

Sherman couldn't bear it any longer. He buckled under the pressure and blurted out that he'd spoken directly to George Washington himself.

Penny blinked in surprise. For a moment she almost believed him. Then reality set in. "Liar!" she mocked him.

Sherman groaned in frustration. He wasn't lying, and there was only one way he could think of to prove it.

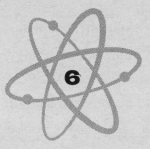

Meanwhile, in the living room, Mr. Peabody was going out of his way to win over the Petersons. He told plenty of jokes and anecdotes, served a gourmet meal, and expertly performed a number of their favorite songs on musical instruments from the piano to the Australian didgeridoo.

Patty Peterson clapped in delight. She turned to her husband, who had managed to keep the sour expression on his face despite Mr. Peabody's best efforts.

"You know what? This has been great," Paul said sarcastically, "but a complete waste of time. Let's get Penny and go ho— Ow-ow-ow!" Mr. Peterson grabbed his back and doubled over in pain.

"Are you all right?" Mr. Peabody asked, concerned.

"This happens whenever he's tense," Patty explained.

Mr. Peabody offered to help. "I'm a licensed chiropractor," he said, approaching Paul. Mr. Peterson shook his head and warned Mr. Peabody not to touch him. He staggered across the living room, clutching his back and howling.

Mr. Peabody took matters into his own paws and gripped Paul by the shoulders. He twisted Mr. Peterson's back this way and that until each vertebra in his spine clicked and popped into place with a loud cracking noise. Suddenly, Paul straightened and blinked in surprise. The pain in his back had completely vanished.

"Peabody! I feel great!" he exclaimed. Paul circled his arms, jogged in place, and danced a jig, giddy with excitement. "You're a miracle worker!"

"I am," Mr. Peabody agreed conspiratorially. From the wide smile on Paul's face, he knew he'd made a breakthrough. It was only a matter of time before he had both Petersons eating out of his paws.

At the same moment that her father was changing his mind about Mr. Peabody, Penny's eyes were popping open in disbelief. She was standing next to Sherman staring into a huge, space-age-style room lined with mirrored panels reflecting the stars, spiral galaxies, and

32

black holes throughout the universe. In the center of the room floated a shiny red sphere that seemed to beckon her with the promise of adventure.

"He calls it the WABAC," Sherman said, pointing to the time machine with a small flourish.

"So where have you gone in it?" Penny asked.

"Not where, Penny, *when*," he answered seriously. When it came to time travel, he was something of an expert.

Penny rolled her eyes. "Okay—*when*, smart guy?"

"Oh . . . 1865, 1776, 1620, 1492," Sherman said casually.

Penny's mouth hung open in astonishment. She blinked and quickly recovered. She wasn't about to let Sherman see how impressed she was. "Can it go back to an hour ago?"

"Why?" asked Sherman.

"Because I could take it home, pretend to be sick, and not come to this lame dinner party," Penny said snidely.

"Ha, ha. Mr. Peabody says you should never use the WABAC to travel to a time when you existed," Sherman explained.

"How come?" Penny asked.

"There'd be two of you," Sherman answered.

Penny considered that possibility for a moment and then said, "Oh. Yeah. I guess the world's not ready for that." She smirked and walked boldly toward the WABAC. "So where should we go first?"

"Mr. Peabody says I'm not allowed to drive it until I'm older," Sherman replied.

"Do you always do everything Mr. Peabody says?" Penny asked.

"Yeah," Sherman said good-naturedly.

"Do you know what that makes you, Sherman?"

"An obedient son?" he asked hopefully.

Penny shook her head. She clapped a not-so-sympathetic hand on Sherman's shoulder and said, "Nope. A *dog*."

A short while later, Mr. Peabody raised his glass to toast with his new friends, the Petersons. Paul and Patty smiled and clinked their glasses with his. They relaxed against the sofa and sipped their drinks happily. All thoughts of pressing charges against Sherman had been forgotten.

Mr. Peabody sighed in relief. He was just about to celebrate the success of his plan when he heard Sherman call to him from the hallway. He excused himself politely and stepped away from the Petersons to speak to his son.

"I've really hit it off with Penny's parents! I think we can file this night under Unqualified Success!" Mr. Peabody said, stepping into the hall.

"I'd hold off on filing it just yet," Sherman mumbled.

"What do you mean?" He looked closely at Sherman and realized instantly that something was wrong. "Where's Penny?" he asked with growing concern.

"Um, ancient Egypt," Sherman said guiltily.

"You used the WABAC? How could you do such a thing?" Mr. Peabody was fuming!

"She called me a liar for saying George Washington never cut down a cherry tree!" Sherman tried to defend himself, but the more he tried to explain, the sillier the whole thing sounded.

"So you took her to see George Washington?" Mr. Peabody asked angrily.

"And a few other people . . . yeah," Sherman confessed.

Just then, Penny's parents walked into the hall. Paul grinned at Mr. Peabody, ready for more fun. But one look at the nervous smile on Mr. Peabody's face told him there was something fishy going on. He also noticed that someone was missing.

"Where's Penny?" Mr. Peterson asked, suddenly suspicious.

"Playing hide-and-seek," Mr. Peabody lied. He might have gotten away with it if Sherman hadn't cried out at the very same moment, "Pooping!"

The Petersons didn't buy that for one minute. They called for Penny and became increasingly worried when there was no answer.

"Where's our daughter?" Paul yelled frantically.

"It's hard to say, Paul. She could be here," Mr. Peabody said, pointing his paw in one direction. "Or here." He pointed in the opposite direction. "Or here." Again, he moved his paw rapidly, pointing from left to right, up and down around the room.

The Petersons followed Mr. Peabody's paw with their eyes. Their gaze bounced from place to place as his paw darted back and forth in a hypnotic rhythm. Within moments, they fell into a trance and stood frozen in place.

Mr. Peabody knew the trance wouldn't last forever. He and Sherman had to find Penny before her parents woke up. There wasn't a moment to lose! Together they raced down the hall to the WABAC and blasted off to ancient Egypt.

7

The hot sun shimmered over the desert sands of ancient Egypt. Great stone pyramids glinted in the afternoon light, and an enormous statue of a sphinx with the head of a human and the body of a lion looked out across the dunes.

Nearby, in the palace of the pharaohs, Penny reclined on an elegant couch. Servants fed her grapes and fanned her with large palm fronds. She sighed in contentment. At last she'd found a time and place where people knew how to treat her in style. So when Sherman stumbled into the palace followed by Mr. Peabody, she wasn't happy to see them at all.

"What are you doing here?" she asked, annoyed.

"We have come to take you home," Mr. Peabody said.

"Who died and made you pharaoh?" asked Penny

sarcastically. She rose from her couch and clapped her hands, summoning her servants. They swirled around her, eager to cater to her every whim. They styled her hair, painted her nails, and covered her in expensive silks and jewels. When they finally stepped aside, Penny was transformed.

"I'm not Penny anymore," she told them. "I'm Princess Hatsheput, precious flower of the Nile."

"Precious, perhaps, but if you think we're going to leave you here, you are most definitely *in denial*," Mr. Peabody said, winking at Sherman because of his pun on Egypt's famous Nile River.

"Ha, ha! In denial!" Sherman laughed. Then his brow wrinkled in confusion. "I don't get it."

Mr. Peabody took Penny by the arm. "Now come along," he said. He was anxious to get back to the present before Penny's parents woke up.

"Unhand her!" a peevish voice shouted.

Mr. Peabody and Sherman turned to see a boy Penny's age being carried into the room. A royal fanfare announced his arrival. He was dressed in the finest garments Sherman had ever seen, and he sat on a golden throne, which rested on the shoulders of servants. A single lock of hair hung from his otherwise bald head.

The boy leapt from his throne and ran to Penny's side. "What's the matter, my sweet little desert blossom? Are these barbarians bothering you?" he asked.

"As a matter of fact, they are," Penny answered.

The boy frowned at Sherman and Mr. Peabody. "Bow, barbarians!" he demanded.

Sherman was shocked to see Mr. Peabody sweep a courteous bow. "Who's that, Mr. Peabody?" he whispered.

"That, Sherman, is the Living Image of Amun—son of Akhnaten, lord of the eighteenth dynasty of the New Kingdom—King Tutankhamen, otherwise known as King Tut," Mr. Peabody explained.

"My boyfriend," Penny added with a snooty smile.

"King Tut is your boyfriend?" Sherman's mouth fell open in shock.

Penny took King Tut's hand and announced that they were going to be married.

"You can't marry this guy! He's . . . he's . . . he's bald!" Sherman sputtered. For some reason, the thought of Penny having a boyfriend made him furious.

"I don't care," Penny said. "I'm gonna have a big fat Egyptian wedding!"

Mr. Peabody remained calm. The news of Penny's

wedding was actually just what he needed to convince her to go home. "Spoiler alert: King Tut dies young. Are you sure you've thought this through?" he asked.

"Oh, trust me, I've thought it through," Penny said, smirking. "I'm getting everything."

Mr. Peabody asked the king's advisor, Ay, to tell Penny exactly what it meant to be married to the pharaoh.

"It means she will be bound to King Tut in eternity through the sacred ceremonies of disembowelment and mummification, as described in the holy texts," Ay explained. He pulled a scroll from his robes and unrolled it to show to Penny. The hieroglyphic drawings were a step-by-step guide to mummification—and it wasn't pretty. Once the king died, his queen was killed, too. Her organs were removed and placed in jars, and then she was turned into a mummy.

Penny immediately realized that marrying the pharaoh wasn't as great as it sounded. There was no way she was going to end up a mummy! "I'm ready to leave with you now," she told Mr. Peabody. Unfortunately, the love-struck boy king had other plans. He nodded to Ay, who declared grandly that the wedding would take place the next day at dawn.

"Mr. Peabody! Sherman! Do something!" Penny

shouted as King Tut and his servants led her away.

"Don't worry, Penny! We'll save you!" Sherman said valiantly.

But saving Penny wasn't going to be easy. Suddenly, the king's guards appeared and dragged Mr. Peabody and Sherman out of the palace. The guards threw them into a dark, dank tomb and rolled a heavy stone slab over the entrance, sealing them inside.

8

The Egyptian tomb was a spooky place. It was pitch-black, cold, and musty. Sherman stood close to Mr. Peabody and grasped his hand in fear.

"Boy, your hand is cold, Mr. Peabody," Sherman whispered in the darkness. He thought it was best to keep his voice down. The tomb was a final resting place for the dead, and he didn't want to wake them.

"That's not my hand, Sherman," Mr. Peabody replied. He found a piece of flint and struck it against a wall, creating sparks. In seconds, he lit a torch. Light flooded the chamber.

Sherman gasped as he realized he was holding the cold, dry hand of an ancient mummy! He jumped back from the figure wrapped in tattered strips of cloth and ran over to Mr. Peabody, who was staring at a string of hieroglyphics painted on the sandstone wall.

Mr. Peabody traced the ancient picture writing with his paw. He studied it closely, looking for any clue that might help them escape. "Hmm, this depicts the god Anubis sailing a boat of Ra to the underworld. It appears the boats of Ra are the key," he reasoned. "We must find them in time to stop the wedding."

Sherman's expression soured at the mention of the wedding. "Well, if you ask me, we should let her marry that guy! They deserve each other," he said, sulking.

Mr. Peabody looked away from the hieroglyphs to cast a quick glance at Sherman. The boy's lower lip was poking out in a surly pout.

"If I didn't know any better, Sherman, I'd say you were jealous," Mr. Peabody observed.

Sherman reeled in surprise and then spluttered, "You think I *like* Penny?"

"Mmm-hmm." Mr. Peabody nodded.

"Gimme a break! It's not like I want to hold her hand or go to the park with her or watch her while she's brushing her hair . . . or anything." Sherman's eyes glazed over as he lapsed into a daydream and his hand reached out to stroke her beautiful blond hair.

"Aha!" Mr. Peabody exclaimed, snapping Sherman

out of his reverie. He found a loose tile in the stone wall and pushed it. The wall rumbled and slid back, revealing a secret passageway.

Mr. Peabody and Sherman ran down the dark corridor, which opened into a vast chamber with high ceilings. The floor was composed of elaborately decorated square tiles, each bearing a hieroglyph.

Sherman was about to step on one of the tiles, but Mr. Peabody held him back. "Careful," he warned.

Mr. Peabody looked closely at the squares and realized he would have to step on them in a certain order. Otherwise, he and Sherman could stumble into a deadly trap. Luckily, the hieroglyphs on each tile showed him the way.

Mr. Peabody leapt from one tile to the next, hopscotching his way across the room. He recited the meaning of each hieroglyph aloud as he jumped so Sherman could follow the pattern. "'The boat . . . of Ra . . . sails straight . . . to . . . day. . . . Take . . . the wrong boat . . . man . . . will pay.'"

Mr. Peabody landed safely in the passageway on the opposite side of the room. "Now it's your turn, Sherman," he called, cautioning him to follow in his exact footsteps.

Sherman was nervous. His palms were sweating, but he knew that sometimes even the bravest explorers got a little sweaty. He jumped out onto the floor squares and spoke the words in a shaky voice. "The boat . . . of Ra . . . sails straight . . . to . . . day. . . . Take . . . the wrong boat . . . man . . . will play."

Just then, Sherman looked down. He'd landed on the wrong tile. "I mean *pay!*" he said, hopping quickly to the right square. But he wasn't fast enough. The tiles around him rumbled ominously with a sound like thunder. They split and cracked, and within moments, the entire tomb started to crumble. Stones fell from the walls, and the floor itself began to disintegrate.

"Run!" Mr. Peabody yelled.

Sherman sprinted the last few feet and dove into the passage where Mr. Peabody was waiting. They raced down the corridor as the floor broke apart behind them, stones slipping away beneath their heels. The passage opened into a cavernous space with two golden boats sitting side by side in the middle of the room. Each boat was docked on a wooden platform in front of a stone chute.

"The boats of Ra!" Mr. Peabody shouted over the roar of crumbling tomb. "One boat is the way out; the other will send us plunging into darkness and certain death!"

"What?" Sherman asked, alarmed.

Mr. Peabody quickly scanned the chamber, looking for the mechanism to launch the boats. His eyes came to rest on a row of three stone blocks, each painted with a sparkling scarab. He studied the blocks for a moment and figured out what he had to do.

"Sherman, get in the boat! As soon as I move these blocks together, it's going to move very fast," he told him.

"Which boat?" Sherman asked. He could barely hear Mr. Peabody over the rumble.

"That one!" Mr. Peabody answered, pointing.

With all the commotion, it was hard for Sherman to see which boat Mr. Peabody was talking about. Chunks of stone dropped from the ceiling, churning up dirt and dust. Sherman sprinted through the falling stones and hopped into the boat on the left.

Mr. Peabody arranged the scarab blocks in the proper order and launched the ships. Both boats rose on their platforms and tipped forward into the chutes. At the last possible moment, Mr. Peabody scrambled through the rubble and jumped into the boat on the right.

"We did it, Sherman!" he said triumphantly. When Sherman didn't answer, Mr. Peabody spun around. The back of his boat was empty!

In the chute across from his, Mr. Peabody watched as the other boat slid into view. Sherman was riding at the helm. When Sherman realized he'd gotten into the "certain death" boat, he panicked. "What should I do, Mr. Peabody?" he called across the growing chasm between the two chutes.

Mr. Peabody quickly came up with a plan. He noticed a length of rope on the floor of his boat and leapt into action. He tied one end of the rope to the mast of his ship and looped the other around his waist. In a daring display of courage, he jumped from his boat and swung out across the chasm.

Mr. Peabody swooped down into Sherman's boat and scooped him up. Together they swung back across the abyss into Mr. Peabody's boat.

Up ahead, both chutes came to a sudden end. Sherman's boat plunged into the deep, dark cavern below, while Mr. Peabody's boat sailed into the air. The ship shot through a narrow tunnel into the bright, hot desert. It crashed into a giant dune in a swirling cloud of sand.

When the sand settled, Mr. Peabody and Sherman climbed to their feet. If they hurried, they'd have just enough time to stop Penny's wedding.

9

The wedding of King Tut and Penny Peterson was a highly anticipated event. The entire village had gathered in the courtyard beside the pharaoh's palace to witness it. In the center of the courtyard, Penny and Tut faced each other on a specially decorated wedding dais. Ay stood between the bride and groom, dressed in his finest ceremonial robes. He bowed and called everyone to attention.

"The sun god Ra commands us to begin the ceremony!" Ay proclaimed.

Penny looked across the crowd of spectators. Royal servants stood guard at the head of each aisle, blocking every escape route. Penny gulped. It looked like she might actually have to go through with the wedding.

After a sacred prayer and a reading of the holy texts,

Ay announced that it was time for the blood oath. Penny's eyes widened in alarm as an attendant approached with the knife used for the ritual. Ay took the knife and held the sharp blade above Penny's palm. She tried to pull away, but several guards stepped forward and forced her to hold out her hand.

"Where blade meets flesh in this sacred rite, we pay tribute to the sun god Ra!" Ay declared.

"Wait!" boomed a menacing voice.

Ay, Penny, and King Tut looked up in wonder. At the edge of the raised dais was a tall stone statue of Anubis, the dog-headed god of death. Smoke billowed from the statue's muzzle, and its eyes glowed like hot coals. The crowd gasped as a deep voice rumbled from the statue's mouth, "This wedding must not continue!"

"Why, Anubis?" the crowd asked, startled.

"Plagues! Plagues!" Anubis roared. "If this marriage pact is sealed, I will shower down upon the land uncountable plagues!"

Penny sighed in relief. The Egyptian god was on her side! She looked carefully at Anubis and realized why. It was no coincidence that the dog-headed statue had learned to speak—she suspected there was a talking dog hidden inside.

"But, Anubis," Ay said, stunned, "the sun god Ra has decreed that this girl is to be the boy king's wife!"

"That's so funny. I was talking to the sun god Ra just the other day, and he told me he'd changed his mind," Anubis replied casually. "Old Flip-Flop Ra, we call him here in the Underworld."

"Really?" Ay blinked, confused. "But it's too late. We've already paid for the catering!"

"Too bad!" Anubis barked angrily. A great ball of flame roared from his mouth, and the wedding guests cowered in fear.

Inside the head of the statue, Mr. Peabody and Sherman proceeded with their clever rescue plan. To make smoke, Sherman worked a bellows over a small fire surrounded by a ring of stones. At the same time, Mr. Peabody spoke into a megaphone to project his voice.

"Deliver the girl to the gates of the city and leave her there, where the gods will retrieve her!" Mr. Peabody commanded. "Only in this manner may the plagues upon this land be avoided."

Ay and King Tut were eager to obey Anubis. They motioned to the royal guards to take Penny to the city gates.

Mr. Peabody watched from inside the statue's

mouth. "More smoke, Sherman," he whispered. "This canine subterfuge is working."

Sherman leaned on the bellows and blew a puff of air across the fire. The blast sent a hot coal hopping from the flames onto Sherman's foot. He howled in pain, kicking the coal away. Unfortunately, it bounced into a pile of straw and instantly set it ablaze.

Sherman tried to smother the fire by stomping on the flames. The statue's mouth filled with thick, heavy smoke, making it hard for them to breathe. Mr. Peabody coughed into the megaphone.

At the sound of the peculiar cough, Ay stopped the guards escorting Penny to the gate. "Anubis, you sound *unwell*," he said, growing suspicious.

"Ahem, well, I have been feeling a little under the weather, but I'm feeling much better now, thank you!" Mr. Peabody replied hurriedly.

The smoke was clearing in the statue's mouth as Sherman put out the fire. He squelched the last of the flames with a mighty stomp. At that moment, the stone beneath Sherman's feet rumbled and cracked. The first cracks were small, but they spread quickly as the rock splintered apart. With a thunderous boom, the statue's lower jaw broke off in one enormous chunk.

"Aaaargh!" Sherman yelled as he and Mr. Peabody tumbled headlong to the ground. They landed in a heap on the wedding dais and scrambled to their feet.

King Tut was not at all pleased to discover he'd been tricked. He ordered his guards to seize the two Anubis impersonators. The guards marched onto the wedding platform, determined to capture them.

Mr. Peabody spotted the statue's stone jaw just a few feet away. Thinking quickly, he maneuvered it to the top of the stairs leading from the dais. He called out to Penny and Sherman to join him, and together they hopped onto the jaw. With a quick push, they were off. They tobogganed down the steps, bowling over guards left and right!

At the bottom of the stairs, the jaw slammed into a wooden ramp, which launched Penny, Sherman, and Mr. Peabody into the air. They flew across the courtyard and landed in a cart of oranges next to a huge stone statue of the sun god Ra.

Sherman was relieved to see the familiar statue surrounded by scaffolding. The WABAC was parked at the very top. If they could reach the time machine before the guards caught them, they could make their escape.

The Egyptian servants hurried after them, with King Tut leading the charge. He rode high on Ay's shoulders in a royal piggyback, calling for the return of his precious desert blossom, Princess Hatsheput.

Penny, Sherman, and Mr. Peabody scrambled out of the orange cart and ran toward the scaffolding. Mr. Peabody helped Penny and Sherman onto a wooden plank held in place by a gnarled length of rope. With King Tut's guards getting closer by the second, Mr. Peabody grabbed the rope in his paws and dashed away from the kids to create a distraction. The guards took the bait and hurled their spears at the clever canine.

Mr. Peabody dodged the pointy weapons with the grace of an Olympic medalist in the long jump—which, fortunately, he happened to be. **Thunk! Thunk!** The spears missed and landed in the wall behind him.

Mr. Peabody looped the rope around the shafts and tugged. The rope snapped, yanking him into the air and hurtling the wooden plank skyward. Penny and Sherman sailed to the top of the statue, colliding with an airborne Mr. Peabody. They landed in a tangle of arms and legs in front of the WABAC.

The three fugitives clambered aboard the time

machine and prepared for immediate takeoff. As Mr. Peabody took the controls, Penny realized she was eager for the trip home. At least in the present, there was no chance of being turned into a mummy!

As the WABAC hurtled through space-time, Mr. Peabody detected a problem among the flashing lights and blinking gauges of the sophisticated time-travel machine.

"All this zipping about the cosmos has drained our power supply," he told Penny and Sherman. "We're going to have to make an unscheduled stop."

The WABAC sputtered to a stop in an Italian village during the Renaissance, a period of enlightenment when art and science flourished all across Europe. Mr. Peabody loved to visit this particular village because his good friend Leonardo da Vinci, the famous inventor and painter, lived there.

But today Leonardo was in a bad mood. "How many times I gotta tell you, Mona Lisa. I can't-a paint-a da picture until you smile!" he howled in frustration as Sherman, Penny, and Mr. Peabody walked into his workshop.

Leonardo's workshop was an inventor's wonderland. Peculiar sketches, paintings, and drawings hung from the walls, and every available corner was stuffed with curious contraptions and abandoned inventions. In the middle of the room, Leonardo stood in front of a half-painted canvas, glaring daggers at a mysterious dark-haired woman. The woman crossed her arms and stuck her tongue out at Leonardo. She absolutely refused to smile.

Mr. Peabody cleared his throat and Leonardo noticed that he had guests. "Peabody, my old friend! What a welcome interruption! Believe-a you me, this-a woman, she make-a me nuts!"

The woman in question, Mona Lisa, chose that exact moment to blow a loud raspberry in Leonardo's face. He turned red with anger and shook his paintbrush at her menacingly.

Before things could get worse, Mr. Peabody stepped in and offered to help. If he could get Mona Lisa to smile for her painting, then Leonardo would help him fix the WABAC's power supply.

According to Mr. Peabody's calculations, getting Mona Lisa to smile wouldn't be difficult. "You see, humor is not immune to the laws of science," he explained. "Using algorithms, we can extrapolate what is universally considered funny, thus producing a formula that is scientifically certain to cause laughter. Case in point: the pratfall."

Mr. Peabody took two steps and then purposefully keeled over and fell flat on his face. "Is everyone amused?" he asked.

No one laughed. In fact, Mona Lisa looked downright bored.

"Hmm, the data was so clear," Mr. Peabody said, puzzled by the fact that his humor formula had failed. He sat up and accidentally bumped into Leonardo's half-finished painting. The canvas wobbled on the easel.

"Don't worry, Mr. Peabody, I got it!" Sherman said, racing toward the painting.

"No, no! Sherman!" Mr. Peabody tried to stop the boy, but he wasn't fast enough. Sherman tripped and fell headlong into the easel. The heavy canvas toppled and smashed Mr. Peabody over the head.

Mr. Peabody staggered to his feet, and everyone

began to laugh. With his head poking through the painting, it looked like his own body had been replaced by Mona Lisa's!

Mona Lisa couldn't keep from giggling. Finally, a smile spread across her lips.

"Perfecto! Hold-a dat smile!" Leonardo shouted, and picked up his paintbrush. He winked at Sherman as he set to work on a new canvas. Mr. Peabody might have been the famous scientist, but it was Sherman who'd discovered the formula for funny.

A short while later, Leonardo and Mr. Peabody were hard at work building a generator that would supply power to the WABAC's fuel cells. Mr. Peabody asked Sherman to help. He thought it would be a good chance for the two of them to spend some father and son time together.

"Okay," Sherman agreed. "So, what do you want me to do?"

"Why don't you fetch the hammer for Mr. da Vinci?" said Mr. Peabody.

Sherman quickly searched the workshop and found a hammer nearby. On his way over to Leonardo, he took a careful look at the contraption they were building. It was made of interlocking wooden cogs and gears with blades that spun slowly like an old-fashioned propeller.

Curious, Sherman looked closer at the mechanism and noticed that one of the cogs was coming loose. It didn't take him long to see why. Mr. Peabody was busy hammering a gear on the other side of the device, and it was knocking the cog out of place.

"Mr. Peabody . . . ," Sherman called, trying to warn him.

"Well, done, Sherman. Very helpful," Mr. Peabody replied absently. He was so absorbed in his work that he wasn't paying attention.

Sherman decided to take matters into his own hands and fix the loose cog himself. He pushed the wooden cog back into place and whacked it with the hammer. The whole contraption shuddered, vibrating with each swing of Sherman's hammer. On the other side of the machine, a huge gear lurched forward and smacked Mr. Peabody in the face.

"Sherman!" Mr. Peabody shouted. But it was Sherman's turn to be absorbed in his work. He kept hammering, accidentally whacking Mr. Peabody with each blow. **"Sherman!"**

At last, Sherman stopped. "Yes, Mr. Peabody?"

"The hammer? Da Vinci?" Mr. Peabody reminded him.

Sherman turned the hammer over to Leonardo and asked if there was anything else he could do to help. Leonardo shook his head politely but emphatically. If Sherman helped any more, the whole machine would fall apart!

Just then, Penny popped her head through the open door of the workshop. "**Psst.** Sherman, let's go explore!" she said.

"I'm supposed to be having father-son time with Mr. Peabody," he replied dutifully.

Penny gave Sherman a mischievous smile. "Wouldn't you rather be having fun with me?"

Sherman blushed and broke into a goofy grin. Penny ducked out the door, and Sherman started after her.

"Sherman! Where are you going?" Mr. Peabody asked. "We need your help here."

"No, we don't!" Leonardo said quickly. "I mean, we can manage somehow. He's a boy, Peabody. Let him have his fun. Let him go."

Before Mr. Peabody could answer, Sherman thanked him and raced from the room. Suddenly, Mr. Peabody felt oddly lonely.

Leonardo saw the expression on his friend's face

Mr. Peabody is an inventor and a genius who also happens to be a dog. He has an adopted son named Sherman.

Mr. Peabody invented a time machine called the WABAC (pronounced "way back") to teach Sherman about important events in history.

Sherman's first day of school feels like an adventure until he meets a girl named Penny Peterson.

Penny is mean to Sherman because he knows more about history than she does.

Mr. Peabody invites the Petersons to dinner . . . without telling Sherman.

When Penny and her parents arrive . . .

. . . Sherman freaks out!

Penny's mom is delighted to meet the famous Mr. Peabody, but Penny's father is not.

Mr. Peabody tells Sherman to be nice to Penny, but warns him not to tell her about the WABAC.

Penny bullies Sherman. She asks him
how he knows so much about history.

Uh-oh! Sherman accidentally tells
Penny about the WABAC.

Sherman takes Penny to see the WABAC. Penny is impressed by the amazing time machine.

Penny convinces Sherman to take her for a ride into the past.

and clapped a hand on his shoulder. "He's-a growing up, Peabody. Like a baby bird, leaving the nest. Isn't it wonderful?" he asked.

Mr. Peabody tried to smile, but it didn't quite work. He wasn't ready for Sherman to leave the nest.

11

Exploring led Penny and Sherman to the attic of Leonardo's workshop. If the downstairs had seemed crowded with inventions, it was nothing compared to the attic. The cavernous room was packed wall to wall with paintings and models and gadgets in different stages of development.

Penny threaded her way through the attic with Sherman right behind her. Both of them stared in wonder at Leonardo's fantastic devices.

"Look at all this stuff," Penny said. "It's old, but it's cool. This guy really is a genius."

She wandered toward the far end of the room and stopped in front of what appeared to be a giant model airplane. The plane was definitely old-fashioned and looked more like a hang glider than a jet. It had a thin wooden frame with two canvas-covered wings and a fanlike tail. Below the wings were a platform with a pilot's seat and what looked like steering controls. The whole contraption was perched on a ramp and attached to an enormous rubber band.

Sherman's eyes grew wide with excitement. He realized he was staring at the prototype for one of Leonardo's most famous inventions: the flying machine.

"Wouldn't it be cool if we could fly it?" Penny whispered.

Sherman nodded. The flying machine practically called out for an adventure, but he had a feeling Mr. Peabody wouldn't approve.

"Well, Mr. Peabody isn't here," Penny said, as if reading his thoughts.

Penny climbed into the pilot's seat of the flying machine. She studied the row of levers in front of her and asked Sherman if he knew how they worked. Despite his growing enthusiasm, Sherman was reluctant to answer. He knew he could get into trouble for touching Leonardo's invention without permission, but he quickly forgot all that once Penny smiled and batted her eyelashes at him.

"The thrust comes from this kinda crossbow-doohickey here," Sherman explained, climbing onto the edge of the platform. He walked Penny through the controls with brainy satisfaction. "Then it shoots along this track until the wind catches the wings."

Penny nodded and listened attentively. "But how do you take off?" she asked innocently.

"You just pull that lever down," Sherman answered.

"This one?" Penny asked, pointing to a foot pedal not far from the steering column. In answer to her question, Sherman stepped on the pedal and discovered that it wasn't so much a pedal as it was a switch. And flipping the switch released the tension on the enormous rubber band attached to the glider. Suddenly, the band snapped forward, launching the flying machine into the air like a giant slingshot.

"AHHHHHHHHHHHHH!" Sherman yelled, clinging to the side of the glider while Penny squealed in delight. The flying machine shot through an open window and out into the sky.

Sherman scrambled into the pilot's seat beside Penny. "This is crazy!" he shouted.

"No, it's not, Sherman. It's fun!" she said, exhilarated.

Penny grabbed the controls and guided the plane over the treetops. From there they could see Leonardo's entire village. As they flew over the town, colored domes and tile roofs could be seen above the trees.

Sherman clapped his hands over his eyes. He could barely look. "We're gonna die!" he wailed.

"Oh, stop being such a party pooper and enjoy it!" Penny said.

After a few moments, Sherman peeked through his fingers. The Italian countryside streaked past in a blur of rolling green hills. Fascinated, he moved his hands from his eyes and sneaked a glance at Penny. Her jaw was set with determination as she steered the flying machine in a wide arc that carried them toward the village square. The wind ruffled her hair, and her eyes were bright with excitement.

Sherman looked away, suddenly shy. It dawned on him that he was sitting very close to Penny, and he blushed to the roots of his hair.

Just then, Penny let go of the controls. "Here, Sherman, *you* fly it," she said.

"What?" Sherman asked, alarmed. "I don't want to fly!"

"Sure you do! It'll be fun." Penny smiled encouragingly.

With no one holding the controls, the flying machine dipped into a nosedive, spiraling toward the ground.

"Seriously, I don't want to!" Sherman protested. He

made the mistake of looking down and saw the ground rushing up to meet them. **"AHHH!** Penny, fly the plane!"

Penny shook her head. "You're going to have to save us!" she insisted.

Sherman gulped. He was scared, but deep down he knew he didn't have a choice. He reached out, grabbed the controls, and pulled back hard on the steering stick. The flying machine lurched out of the dive, narrowly avoiding the ground.

Sherman and Penny sighed in relief, but they had no time to celebrate. Ahead, the tall stone steeple of a cathedral reared up in front of them. There was no avoiding it! Sherman glanced up at the flying machine's canvas wings and noticed two small handles hanging down. Instinctively, he pulled the handles and the wings collapsed, allowing the glider to slip through the steeple's open windows like a thread through the eye of a needle.

The flying machine sailed beneath the beams of the cathedral's high ceilings and out a window on the other side. Sherman opened the wings and caught a draft of air that sent them soaring toward the nearby river.

"See? You got this!" Penny said brightly.

"You're right. I *have* got this!" Sherman replied

happily. He was doing it! He was actually flying!

Sherman leaned forward in the pilot's seat with a growing sense of confidence. He guided the plane through several loops, weaving in and out of the clouds, and then dipped low over the calm surface of the river.

Penny whooped, delighted, as she leaned down and trailed her fingers across the water. She smiled at Sherman, impressed with his newfound confidence, and splashed him playfully. Sherman beamed. He was having the time of his life.

Meanwhile, Leonardo and Mr. Peabody had just finished their repairs to the WABAC when they noticed an unusual shape streaking across the sky.

"Hey, look, Peabody, it's my flying machine!" Leonardo said, surprised.

Mr. Peabody narrowed his eyes and peered up at the flier as it swooped in their direction. Shocked, he spotted Sherman at the controls!

"Sherman? What are you doing?" he called, exasperated.

"I'm flying!" Sherman shouted gleefully.

"But, Sherman, you don't know how to fly!" Mr. Peabody called out.

"I don't?" asked Sherman.

"No!" Mr. Peabody yelled emphatically.

Sherman's eyes widened. He suddenly felt as if he had no idea what he was doing. It was enough to scare him out of his wits. Frightened, he lost control of the flying machine and it plummeted toward the ground.

"Turn, Sherman! Lean!" Mr. Peabody shouted. But it was too late for advice. The glider plunged downward and crashed in a tree outside Leonardo's workshop. Mr. Peabody and Leonardo rushed over to the crash site in time to see Penny untangle herself from the broken branches and shimmy to the ground.

All three of them searched for Sherman in the snarl of twisted tree limbs.

"Sherman! Sherman! Are you okay?" called Penny anxiously.

There was no answer.

After a tense moment of silence, leaves rustled and Sherman's head popped out from between the branches. His glasses sat crooked on his nose and his hair was a mess, but otherwise, he was unharmed. In fact, he was smiling.

"That was fantastic!" Sherman exclaimed. He was exhilarated.

Mr. Peabody was glad Sherman wasn't hurt, but he wasn't exactly happy with him. The boy had taken Leonardo's flying machine and flown it without permission. He turned to Leonardo, expecting to find a frown on the inventor's face, but instead he was smiling from ear to ear.

"Can you believe it? My flying machine, it's-a work!" Leonardo said, thrilled. "Sherman, you are the first-a flying man!"

Sherman's chest puffed up with pride. Maybe now Mr. Peabody would let him fly the WABAC. But one look at his father's face told him that flying was out of the question. As Mr. Peabody ushered him on board the newly charged WABAC, he knew it was more likely that he was grounded.

12

With the WABAC zooming through space on a course set for home, Mr. Peabody wasted no time in calling a family meeting. Penny wasn't exactly family, but she insisted on being present. Mr. Peabody glared at her and then turned to Sherman. "Stop letting this girl get you into trouble!" he barked.

"What? Like this is all supposed to be my fault now?" Penny asked, narrowing her eyes.

"Yes!" Mr. Peabody shouted. "Ever since Sherman made your acquaintance, it has been one disaster after another!"

"What are you talking about? Sherman flew a plane! He was amazing!" Penny yelled.

Sherman's eyes lit up. Penny was right! "Yeah, Mr. Peabody, I was amazing!"

Mr. Peabody gritted his teeth in frustration. He paced angrily in front of the WABAC's window. Stars and planets whisked by behind him. Abruptly, he stopped pacing and pointed at Penny. "I have enough on my plate with Sherman to keep me busy for a hundred lifetimes without you turning him into a hooligan!"

"It's not my fault he's a hooligan!" Penny objected.

"Yeah, it's not her fault I'm a hooligan!" Sherman echoed. He folded his arms across his chest stubbornly.

"Well, it certainly is not my fault!" Mr. Peabody protested. "I've spent the last seven years teaching Sherman good judgment!"

Penny harrumphed and placed her hands on her hips. "If you're such a good parent, why is Miss Grunion trying to take Sherman away from you?"

Sherman froze. All the color drained from his face. "Is that true?" he asked.

"It's . . . it's complicated," Mr. Peabody answered. It was hard for him to see the hurt look on Sherman's face. He looked out the window into space and suddenly gasped in alarm.

"It's a black hole!" Mr. Peabody shouted.

A swirling vortex of darkness hovered in front of the WABAC. It sucked the ship toward itself with the steady pull of a tractor beam. Mr. Peabody raced to the controls with Sherman and Penny right behind him.

"What's a black hole?" Penny asked nervously.

"A black hole is a region in space-time with such intense gravity that nothing—not even light—can escape!" Mr. Peabody explained. "If I can't pull us out of here, we're going to be smashed to smithereens!"

Mr. Peabody frantically flipped switches, cranked dials, and slapped levers on the WABAC's control panel. The time machine groaned in protest, straining to pull out of the black hole's gravitational field.

Sherman was too mad to be scared. "Why didn't you tell me Miss Grunion was trying to take me away from you?" he yelled at Mr. Peabody over the roar of the ship's engines.

"Because I didn't want you to worry!" Mr. Peabody answered. Sherman gave him a look that said he didn't believe it for one minute. "Okay, because I didn't think you were capable of handling it!" Mr. Peabody admitted.

Sherman glowered. He was furious. "From now on you tell me what's going on when it comes to me!" he demanded.

Mr. Peabody didn't have time to argue. He could

discuss Miss Grunion with Sherman later. Right now he needed to figure out how to save the ship and everyone in it. Sherman's anger would have to wait.

"Sit, Sherman!" Mr. Peabody barked.

"You can't talk to me like that," Sherman muttered angrily. "I'm not a dog."

Mr. Peabody's ears swiveled in Sherman's direction. He turned away from the controls, momentarily forgetting the huge black hole that was just seconds away from engulfing them. "What did you say?"

"I SAID YOU CAN'T TALK TO ME LIKE THAT! I'M NOT A DOG!" Sherman screamed.

Mr. Peabody could barely believe his ears. If it weren't for his supersensitive canine hearing, he would have thought he'd heard wrong. But Sherman had in fact said the one thing that was guaranteed to make him lose his temper. "No, you're not!" Mr. Peabody roared. "You're just a **VERY BAD BOY**!"

Sherman's face crumpled. His bottom lip quivered, and a tear rolled down his cheek. Mr. Peabody instantly regretted his words and wished he could take them back.

He never got the chance.

The WABAC's engines shuddered and howled in

protest. The ship's emergency thrusters kicked into high gear. The WABAC narrowly escaped the gaping maw of the black hole, but the backlash sent the ship and its crew hurtling into the time vortex with no end in sight!

13

The WABAC tumbled end over end, bouncing through time and space. After what seemed like an eternity, the time machine skidded to a halt. Inside the ship, Mr. Peabody was finally able to pull himself to his feet. He switched on a flashlight and immediately began looking for Sherman and Penny. He found Penny but discovered that Sherman had run off as soon as the WABAC had landed.

"I can't believe he ran away," Mr. Peabody said, frustrated. He raised his flashlight and peered into the night. He could just make out the silhouette of a walled city in the distance. In front of the city gates stood a familiar shape—a giant wooden horse on wheels.

"Where are we, anyway?" Penny asked, following him out of the WABAC.

Mr. Peabody sighed with worry as he realized where they were. "We're on the brink of one of history's most ferocious conflicts," he explained. "The Trojan War."

Inside the wooden horse, King Agamemnon of Greece was secretly hiding with an entire army of Greek soldiers. As soon as the Trojans opened the city gates and took the horse inside, the army would climb out and attack.

Agamemnon rallied his troops as they prepared for battle. "How we doing, heroes of Greece? Feeling good? Feeling strong?" the king asked cheerfully. He walked down the line of soldiers, patting each one on the back and slapping them high fives. At the end of the line, he reached the smallest soldier, a new recruit. They had had to give him a new name to make him sound a little more Greek. "Ready to get to the field, Shermanus?" Agamemnon asked.

"Sure thing, Mr. Agamemnon," Sherman replied. He liked his new name, and he liked the Greek soldiers. They treated him like a grown-up, like one of the gang. They'd even given him his own set of armor so he could join them in battle. The armor was a little too big for him, but he didn't mind. He could handle it.

Suddenly, there was a knock on the side of the wooden horse. King Agamemnon opened the hatch and looked down to see one of his soldiers, Odysseus, standing beside a small statue of a wooden horse. It looked just like the horse they were hiding inside.

"Someone left this for us," Odysseus explained.

"A present. Nice!" Agamemnon whispered excitedly. He motioned to Odysseus to bring the gift horse inside. As soon as the horse came through the hatch, the head popped off and Mr. Peabody and Penny climbed out. Shocked, the Greeks soldiers drew their swords. "Whoa! I did not see that coming!" the king admitted.

Mr. Peabody stepped forward bravely. "I've come for Sherman," he declared.

Sherman folded his arms across his chest and sulked. He was still upset with Mr. Peabody for not telling him about Miss Grunion. He didn't want to go anywhere with his dad. "Sorry, Mr. Peabody, I've joined the Greek army," he said.

"Shermanus is one of us now," the Greek general announced. "He took an oath."

"He's seven!" Mr. Peabody pointed out.

Agamemnon looked Sherman straight in the eye. "Your dad may not think you're ready to become a man,

Shermanus, but we do," the king said earnestly.

"Yeah!" the soldiers hollered in support. They hooted loudly and stomped their feet.

Sherman stood proudly in his oversized Greek armor and pushed his helmet back off his forehead. The helmet was way too big for him and kept sliding down over his glasses. "Yeah, Mr. Peabody, now I'll show you what I can handle," he said boldly.

"Sherman, I'm concerned that you haven't thought this through. This is war. Do you realize what is about to happen?" Mr. Peabody asked.

Just then, the wooden horse began to roll forward. The Trojans were pulling it inside the gates of the city. Agamemnon and the other soldiers gathered their weapons and lined up in front of the hatch, ready to begin the invasion.

Sherman took his place beside the soldiers. He squared his shoulders, determined to prove himself.

Mr. Peabody's brow furrowed with concern. "Sherman, I absolutely forbid you to fight in the Trojan War!" he said firmly.

"That's not fair! All my friends are fighting in the Trojan War!" Sherman complained.

"Sherman, it's dangerous!" Mr. Peabody protested.

"I'm wearing a helmet!" Sherman yelled.

Suddenly, King Agamemnon let out a fierce battle cry. The Greek soldiers charged through the hatch and climbed down into the streets of the city. Sherman took one last look at Mr. Peabody and dashed after them.

14

The battle raged through the streets of Troy, with the Greek soldiers squaring off against the Trojans. Swords clashed, fists flew, and arrows zipped through the air as the men grappled with each other. Sherman ran straight into the heart of the battle.

"Eat my bronze, you Trojan dogs!" he shouted, striking a threatening pose.

A burly Trojan soldier spun around and growled fiercely at him. Sherman gulped, frightened. He knew he had two options: stay and fight or run away. In this case, faced with a towering solder nearly three times his size, he chose to run away. As the son of a canine supergenius, he thought it was the smarter choice.

Sherman dropped his sword and ran screaming across the battlefield. He picked a path through the crowd of Greeks and Trojans busy huffing, puffing, and knocking each other to the ground. He glanced swiftly over his shoulder and saw the Trojan soldier close on his heels, snorting and bellowing like an enraged bull. As Sherman scrambled through the streets of Troy, he realized that Mr. Peabody was right—war was dangerous even if you were wearing a helmet!

In fact, one helmet did more harm than good. Sherman tripped over a stray helmet and fell to his knees. The angry soldier saw his advantage and leapt forward, drawing his sword. Sherman knew that if he didn't think of something quickly, he was finished.

Suddenly, he got a brilliant idea. He fished around beneath his armor and found the whistle Mr. Peabody had given him on his first day of school. Sherman blew into the whistle frantically. It was his only hope.

Just as the Trojan soldier lifted his sword to deliver a mighty blow, Mr. Peabody emerged from the fighting. With a well-timed karate chop, he knocked the sword from the soldier's hand and then conked him on the head. The Trojan fell to the ground.

Sherman exhaled in relief. He knew now that he wasn't cut out for battle. Like his dad, he was more of a thinker than a fighter. Mr. Peabody took him by the arm and led him carefully through the fighting back to the wooden horse.

"This is why I ask you to obey me, Sherman—because I'm your father, and it's my job to keep you safe!" Mr. Peabody explained.

"But how can you keep me safe if Miss Grunion is trying to take me away from you?" Sherman asked.

Mr. Peabody turned to look Sherman directly in the eye. "That's not your problem, Sherman. Let me worry about that," he said.

At the foot of the wooden horse, Sherman and Mr. Peabody began to climb toward the hatch. Penny was waiting for them inside, ready to return to the WABAC. Just as Sherman reached the top, the wall of a nearby temple collapsed. The crumbling stone smashed against the side of the wooden horse, causing the horse to begin rolling. Mr. Peabody and Sherman were thrown off balance. As the horse gained momentum, they slipped and tumbled to the ground.

"Penny!" Sherman yelled, alarmed, as the horse rumbled through the city. He jumped to his feet, ready to dash after Penny, but Mr. Peabody stopped him with a look that said he had a plan.

Mr. Peabody's eyes darted across the battlefield, rapidly examining the scene. He noticed two very important things that would go a long way toward rescuing Penny: a horse grazing casually at the edge of the battlefield, and a grappling hook. After a brief calculation determining the speed and velocity of the wooden horse, Mr. Peabody leapt into action.

He grabbed Sherman and raced to the grazing horse. Father and son scrambled onto the horse's back and took off at a gallop. In the distance, they could see the Trojan horse as it trundled across the battlefield toward the steep cliffs just outside the city.

Mr. Peabody guided his horse through the fighting with Sherman seated behind him. They galloped alongside a pair of Trojan soldiers, and when they were close enough, Mr. Peabody deftly plucked the grappling hook from their grasp.

"I'll take that!" he said, winking. He spurred his horse away from the shocked soldiers, heading straight for a flight of stairs that led to the top of the city walls.

The wooden horse rapidly picked up speed. Fighting soldiers dove out of its path as it barreled through the streets. Mr. Peabody urged his horse up the flight of stairs and galloped along the top of the city walls in pursuit. He fastened the claw end of the grappling hook to the sturdy stone barrier, gathering the attached rope in his paws. Sherman held his breath. He watched Mr. Peabody tie a giant loop in the end of the rope and swing it above his head like a cowboy at a rodeo.

As the Trojan horse bowled through the gates beneath the city walls, Mr. Peabody hurled the rope through the air and lassoed the horse's tail. Within seconds, the rope tightened and the huge statue ground to a stop, teetering unsteadily over the edge of the cliffs.

Sherman breathed a sigh of relief. He and Mr. Peabody jumped off the horse and slid down the rope as if they were on a zip line. They landed on the back of the Trojan horse with a loud thud.

"You did it, Mr. Peabody!" Penny exclaimed gratefully.

"Indeed, Penny. Now come along. We must get to the WABAC," said Mr. Peabody.

Penny pulled herself up through the hatch, but her dress got caught on a nail in the wooden boards. She was stuck! Eager to help, Sherman lunged toward her.

"Sherman, no!" Mr. Peabody shouted. He reached out to stop his son, but he wasn't quick enough. As Sherman rushed to Penny's side, his weight tipped the delicate balance of the wooden horse. The horse tilted in the wrong direction and leaned heavily over the cliff's edge.

With seconds to spare, Mr. Peabody jumped hard on a loose plank in the floor. The opposite end of the plank sprang up beneath Penny and Sherman and launched them both clear of the horse. They landed on the ground and rolled to their feet just in time to see the horse slide over the cliff with Mr. Peabody still inside! It plummeted into the ocean, crashing against the rocks below.

"Mr. Peabody! Mr. Peabody!" Sherman called desperately. He peered over the edge of the cliff in horror. All he could see were the shattered pieces of the horse drifting lazily against the rocks in the ocean.

Penny stared down beside him. "Nobody could have survived that. Not even Mr. Peabody," she said sadly.

"Oh, Mr. Peabody! What should I do?" Sherman heaved a heavy sigh. He covered his face with his hands.

"There's nothing you can do, Sherman," Penny whispered gently. "I just want to go home."

"Home?" Sherman asked. He dropped his hands from his face and snapped to attention. "That's it!" he said eagerly, his eyes gleaming with excitement. "I have an idea! Come on!" He took Penny's hand and ran back to the spot where the WABAC had landed.

"What are we gonna do?" Penny asked.

"We're going home," Sherman said confidently. "There's only one person who can help us, and that's Mr. Peabody."

"What are you talking about?" asked Penny skeptically. "How is that even possible?"

"We've got a time machine, Penny," Sherman explained with a grin. "I can set it so that we'll get home when Mr. Peabody is still there!"

"But I thought you're not supposed to go back to a time when you existed?" Penny said warily.

"What choice do we have?" Sherman replied. They climbed on board the WABAC, and he expertly programmed the machine to take them back to Mr. Peabody's dinner party.

As Sherman pressed the red launch button, Penny considered the possibility that where they were going there could be two Shermans. She shook her head—the world definitely wasn't ready for that!

When Penny and Sherman arrived back at the penthouse, Mr. Peabody's dinner party was in full swing. They climbed out of the WABAC and tiptoed down the hallway to the living room. Sounds of laughter and witty conversation drifted out into the hall. Sherman and Penny peeked inside to see Mr. Peabody entertaining the Petersons.

Sherman smiled, happy to see that his plan had worked. Mr. Peabody was still there—only this Mr. Peabody was from the past. He didn't know anything about their recent travels in the WABAC. It was up to Sherman and Penny to tell him.

"Mr. Peabody, can we talk to you for a second?" Sherman whispered.

Mr. Peabody nodded and excused himself from the Petersons, stepping into the hall. "I've really hit it off with Penny's parents! I think we can file this night under Unqualified Success!" he said enthusiastically.

"I'd hold off on filing it just yet," Sherman and Penny said in unison. "What do you mean?" Mr. Peabody asked, studying the kids closely. They were both covered in dust and looked as though they had tumbled from the pages of a history book. Sherman was wrapped in a ragged toga, wearing Greek armor that was much too big for him, and Penny was also dressed in Grecian garb. Mr. Peabody frowned as he put the pieces together. "You used the WABAC."

"I did! I know! It's terrible!" Sherman confessed. He told Mr. Peabody everything, from Penny's crazy Egyptian wedding to Leonardo's flying machine to the Trojan War. "And then you died in ancient Troy!"

"Died? I have a hard time believing that," said Mr. Peabody skeptically.

"It's true!" Sherman insisted. "But now you're here and everything's going to be okay."

Mr. Peabody frowned. He realized he had a bigger problem on his paws. "I told you never to come back to a time when you existed because there'd be two of you!"

"Yeah, but the other one of me is still in ancient Egypt, losing Penny," Sherman said, pleased with himself.

Suddenly, the three of them heard footsteps approaching, and the other Sherman—the one from the dinner party—rounded the corner. Toga Sherman realized he had miscalculated. He and Penny had arrived just as Past Sherman was about to ask Mr. Peabody for help. Past Sherman stopped abruptly and gasped when he came face to face with . . . himself.

"AHHHHHH!" Both Shermans were shocked.

"Who are you?" Past Sherman asked, startled.

"He's you but from another time," Mr. Peabody explained.

Past Sherman wrinkled his brow in confusion. "But I thought you said never to come back to a time when you existed—"

"Exactly." Mr. Peabody fixed the Sherman from ancient Greece with a pointed look.

"I know, I know." Toga Sherman sighed. "But what was I supposed to do? Mr. Peabody died in ancient Troy!"

"Died? I have a hard time believing that." Past Sherman snorted in disbelief.

"Thank you!" Mr. Peabody said. He couldn't understand why everyone thought he had died. He was a supergenius. He could think his way out of anything.

Penny propped her hands on her hips. "What are we going to do?" she asked. In her opinion, having two Shermans was having one Sherman too many.

"Well, for starters, both Shermans can't stay here!" Mr. Peabody told them.

"Why? We could get bunk beds!" Past Sherman said eagerly.

"I was thinking the same thing!" Toga Sherman agreed.

"That's so weird!" Past Sherman exclaimed. "It's like we're twins!"

Toga Sherman nodded enthusiastically. He was starting to like this Past Sherman kid—after all, he was pretty handsome. Toga Sherman raised his hand and leaned in to give his past self a high five. A bright bolt of electricity zipped between the two of them, giving them a jolt.

"Careful! Don't get too close! This situation is putting too much strain on the space-time continuum!" Mr. Peabody warned. He stepped between the two Shermans and held them apart, worried. He had to come up with a solution, and fast! Under no circumstances could he let Penny's parents find out what was going on. If they learned the truth, they would press charges and Miss Grunion would take Sherman away for sure. Just then, Paul and Patty Peterson popped their heads into the hallway. Past Sherman ducked quickly out of sight before Penny's parents spotted him.

"Hey Pea-buddy!" Paul said cheerily. "Patty and I are working up an appetite!"

Mr. Peabody grinned uneasily and cast a nervous glance around the room, hoping that Past Sherman had found a place to hide.

"Hey, what's with the getups?" Patty asked, noticing the kids' strange costumes.

Penny and Toga Sherman exchanged a worried look. Thinking quickly, she draped an arm around his shoulder and said, "Toga party!"

Patty Peterson clapped her hands and whooped delightedly, while Paul suggested they move the party back into the living room.

"No!" Mr. Peabody shouted abruptly. Out of the corner of his eye he saw Past Sherman standing behind

Penny's parents. "I mean, it's so fun . . . right here! To-ga! To-ga!" he chanted, distracting them while Past Sherman scurried toward the penthouse elevator. He was just about to press the call button when the elevator arrived—**DING!**

Past Sherman ducked into the shadows as the elevator doors opened to reveal Miss Grunion.

16

"**M**iss Grunion! How delightful!" Mr. Peabody gushed enthusiastically. But he was secretly terrified. The bothersome woman had picked the worst possible moment to inspect his home.

Miss Grunion stepped into the penthouse and looked around suspiciously. She saw that the Petersons were there and knew Mr. Peabody was up to something. It was only a matter of time before she got to the bottom of it.

"I think you'll find that everything is tip . . . toe!" said Mr. Peabody as Past Sherman tiptoed from the shadows and sneaked behind Miss Grunion into the living room. "Tip-top! Tip-tip-tip-tip-top!" he corrected himself.

Miss Grunion ignored Mr. Peabody's nervous outburst and stepped around him, headed for the living room. "I don't know what your game is, Peabody, but I have an inspection to finish," she said sternly.

Panicked, Mr. Peabody leapt in front of her. "Of course, of course!" he said soothingly. "Why don't you start over here . . . or here . . . or here?" He moved his paw back and forth in a mesmerizing rhythm. It was the same trick he'd used to put the Petersons into a trance, only it didn't work on Miss Grunion.

"Stop waving your hands around," she said, annoyed.

Unfortunately, Mr. Peabody's trick worked a little too well on Past Sherman. Mesmerized, the boy stumbled out of his hiding place in the living room and fell flat on his back.

Miss Grunion and the Petersons reeled in shock. They looked from one Sherman to the other, absolutely baffled.

Paul Peterson used his fingers to take a quick head count. "**Dos Shermanos?** What's going on here, Peabody?" he asked.

"Well . . . you see . . . that's Sherman's twin brother, Herman," he lied quickly. "Say hello, Herman."

Past Sherman climbed to his feet and shook his head, coming out of his trance. "Hello, Herman," he said obediently.

Miss Grunion frowned. She didn't believe the phony

story one bit. "Is that true?" she asked Past Sherman.

Before he could answer, he was interrupted by the sound of the penthouse elevator—**DING!** The doors slid open, and this time Mr. Peabody stepped out—a *second* Mr. Peabody. He wore a dingy toga and a battered Trojan helmet and looked a bit dusty, as if he had been on a very long trip. "No, the truth is . . . I have a time machine," he confessed. "I call it the WABAC."

Toga Sherman could not have been happier to see him. "You didn't die!" he said gladly.

"Of course I didn't die!" said Trojan Peabody.

"Hey, how did you get back?" asked Toga Sherman.

"Well, after a few failed experiments, I hit upon a combination of bone, stone, and yak fat and constructed a rudimentary WABAC," Trojan Peabody explained. "If at first you don't succeed, *Troy, Troy* again."

Past Peabody wasn't impressed. "How could you let this happen?" he said to his other self. "My plan was foolproof—"

"But it wasn't childproof. It turns out raising a boy is more complicated than you thought!" Trojan Peabody explained.

Miss Grunion huffed and folded her arms across her chest. She knew that this couldn't possibly be a good environment for a growing boy. "I knew I'd uncover something unnatural, but I had no idea I was going to be presented with such clear-cut evidence of . . . **weirdness**," she said warily.

"Not weirdness, Miss Grunion—**science**!" Past Peabody said, trying to put a positive spin on the situation.

Trojan Peabody stepped forward and offered to set everything right by using the WABAC to return everyone to their proper timelines. But Miss Grunion felt that things had gone far enough already. She took both Shermans by the hand, determined to remove them from the home!

"No, don't! Miss Grunion, please!" Penny begged. "This is all my fault. I started it!" She turned to the Shermans to apologize. "I'm sorry I picked on you, Sherman. I'm sorry I called you a dog!"

"You have nothing to apologize for, Penny," Miss Grunion said firmly. "A dog should not have been allowed to adopt a boy in the first place. Come along." She pulled both Shermans away from Mr. Peabody, dragging them toward the door.

"Miss Grunion, don't," Mr. Peabody warned her.

The two Shermans struggled to break free of her

grip. They kicked and twisted and finally slipped out of her grasp. Unfortunately, they stumbled and fell smack into each other!

That made the universe very unhappy! The minute one Sherman tripped into the other Sherman, electricity crackled and the entire building shook!

17

It was the oddest stumble anyone had ever seen. When Past Sherman and Toga Sherman tried to climb to their feet, they realized they were stuck together. In fact, they were more than stuck. They were melting into one another! One boy's hand sank into the other's nose, and one boy's foot stuck to the other boy's kneecap. The Shermans were attached to each other like glue, and more electricity crackled as they began to fuse!

"What's happening?" Penny screamed.

Both Peabodys looked on in horror. This was exactly what they'd been afraid of. The laws of physics had been stretched to the limit, and now they were breaking. The universe knew that there should only be one Sherman in one place at one time, so now it was trying to squeeze the two of them back together.

"Mr. Peabody! Help!" the Shermans cried. By now they had blended into a gooey mess with multiple arms and two legs and one terrible head with four eyes!

The Peabodys rushed forward and tried to pull the sticky Shermans apart, but they were sucked into the roiling mass of morphing body parts.

"AHHHHHHHH!" came a strangled scream from the tumbling ball of flailing limbs and cosmic goo formerly known as Sherman and Peabody.

A dangerous rumbling sound built beneath the living room floor, and the lights in the building flickered on and off at an alarming rate. Penny hugged her parents tightly and turned her face away.

The gooey mass writhed and shuddered, sparking arcs of electricity, until it finally exploded with a loud **boom!** Shock waves knocked everyone to the floor.

A few moments later, Miss Grunion and the Petersons pulled themselves to their feet. They had no idea what to expect when the dust settled, and they certainly weren't expecting to see anything so . . . normal. Now there was only one Sherman and one Mr. Peabody, and there was nothing gooey about them.

"I don't know what just happened here, but I know it was wrong! **Very wrong!**" Miss Grunion said, revolted.

"Miss Grunion, please," Mr. Peabody begged. "Let's sit down and discuss this matter like two reasonable—"

"People?" she asked pointedly, looking the literate dog up and down.

"Adults," Mr. Peabody answered.

But Miss Grunion refused to discuss the matter further. She took Sherman by the hand and pulled him toward the elevator.

"Miss Grunion, please don't! I beg of you! Don't take my boy!" Mr. Peabody pleaded.

Sherman looked sadly at his father and tried to run back to him, but Miss Grunion jerked him roughly to her side.

"Ow! You're hurting me!" Sherman shrieked.

That was the last straw for Mr. Peabody. All the logic and science in the world flew right out the window when he saw Miss Grunion hurting his son. It didn't matter that he was a supergenius, or a Nobel Prize winner, or an Olympic gold medalist. It didn't matter that he'd invented a time machine. It didn't even matter that he was a dog. What mattered was that he was Sherman's father, and he wasn't about to let anyone hurt his son.

Mr. Peabody, the world's smartest (and only) literate

dog, did a very bad thing. He bared his teeth, opened wide, and **bit** Miss Grunion!

It was the bite heard round the world—the bite that in ancient Troy would have launched a thousand ships. Penny and the Petersons reeled in shock. Sherman's eyes popped out in surprise. Even Miss Grunion was momentarily stunned, until her shock dissolved into a self-satisfied grin. But no one was more shocked than Mr. Peabody.

Miss Grunion pulled out her cell phone and immediately dialed the police to report the bite.

"Mr. Peabody, what are we going to do?" Sherman whispered worriedly.

Mr. Peabody, the supergenius, was out of ideas— except one.

"RUN!" he shouted.

Mr. Peabody ran for the penthouse elevator and dove inside with Sherman and Penny close behind. The door slammed shut just as they heard Miss Grunion yell, "He's kidnapping the children!"

Mr. Peabody leaned forward and hurriedly punched the button to take them to the WABAC room.

"I know I told you never to bite, Sherman," Mr. Peabody said. "But there's no way I was going to let that woman take you away from me!"

Sherman looked at his dad and smiled. He couldn't have been prouder to have a dog for a father. "That's okay, Mr. Peabody. Everybody makes mistakes sometimes—even me," Sherman said, grinning.

Mr. Peabody smiled at his son, wondering exactly when the boy had become so wise.

The elevator doors opened and Mr. Peabody, Sherman, and Penny raced along the corridor to the WABAC. They quickly climbed on board the time machine.

"And now to return to our proper timeline and erase this mess!" Mr. Peabody announced. He tapped in a series of complicated sequences on the navigation console and then pressed the launch button.

The WABAC's engines revved powerfully. But suddenly, just as the ship was about to take flight, the console sparked and the engines powered down.

"What's wrong?" Sherman asked.

Mr. Peabody carefully checked the instrument panel. "Oh dear," he said with a sigh. "The WABAC can't seem to find a wormhole. We can't go back to the past!"

Seconds later, Penny, Sherman, and Mr. Peabody heard footsteps in the corridor outside the WABAC room. The police had arrived, and they were running down the hall along with Miss Grunion and the Petersons.

"That dog's got my daughter!" Paul Peterson yelled.

Inside the WABAC, Mr. Peabody worked hurriedly on the ship's computer.

"Well, we have to go somewhere!" Penny said desperately. Mr. Peabody looked up from his work. He realized that Penny was right—escaping was the most important thing. Swiftly, he prepared to take off. A large panel in the roof of the penthouse slid open, revealing the sky. Mr. Peabody punched the launch button again, and this time, instead of traveling into the past, the WABAC took to the skies in the present.

19

The WABAC zoomed across through the clouds with Mr. Peabody at the helm. He piloted the ship skillfully between the tall buildings of New York City. A dark, swirling vortex had opened up in the sky very close to Mr. Peabody's penthouse. The clouds churned and rumbled, and lightning forked on the horizon.

Mr. Peabody looked at the roiling sky with a sinking feeling. He knew it was more than just bad weather. "Our cosmic doubles colliding must have ripped a hole in the space-time continuum," he said.

Just then, something hit the WABAC's windshield— **THUMP!** It was Leonardo da Vinci! The Renaissance man had unexpectedly dropped from the sky!

"Hey-a, Peabody!" Leonardo said in his heavy Italian accent. Penny and Sherman stared in surprise as the famous inventor slipped off the windshield and disappeared.

PLUNK! There was another loud sound as Robespierre made contact with the glass. His face was smushed against the windshield in a rubbery grimace. "I will get you, dog!" he shouted before slipping out of sight.

PLONK! This time King Tut appeared. "Penny, my bride!" he yelled as he slid off the glass.

"We really need to get back to the past!" Mr. Peabody said, concerned.

"Looks like the past is coming to us," Sherman replied.

Meanwhile, Miss Grunion, the Petersons, and the cops were following the WABAC from the ground in a police car. They sped through the streets of the city in hot pursuit of the shiny red time machine.

"Follow that orb!" Miss Grunion shouted.

Suddenly, the air crackled and seemed to split apart! A giant wooden horse fell out of the swirling vortex in the sky and landed right in front of the police car. The impact was so hard, it sent the car flying into the air!

A hatch opened in the rear end of the Trojan horse. King Agamemnon poked his head out just in time to see the flying police car. It was headed straight for him!

"Arghh!" he shouted, ducking back inside.

The police car smashed through the rear of the wooden horse and skidded to a stop inside. Dazed from the crash, Miss Grunion, the Petersons, and the police climbed out of the car.

Agamemnon flipped open the hatch again to investigate. He came face to face with Miss Grunion and reared back in horror. "What sort of creature are you?" he asked. "Are you a gorgon? A cyclops?"

"The name's Grunion," she answered, offended.

"It talks!" Agamemnon screamed, slamming the hatch shut.

Miss Grunion shook her head in disgust. One glance at the city streets told her that the Greek king wasn't the last historical figure she'd meet today. The streets were practically crawling with people who'd fallen out of the hole that had opened up in the sky.

All history had broken loose, and she knew just who to blame.

20

New York was a big city, and the people who lived there were used to seeing some unusual things, but they had never seen anything quite like this. The past was literally pouring into the present!

Albert Einstein, the famous physicist, was seen jaywalking on 72nd Street. At 125th Street, Marie Antoinette was seen chasing a cupcake truck. In Midtown, Leonardo da Vinci sped through Times Square in a flashy Italian sports car, and Sigmund Freud, the father of psychoanalysis, strolled through the East Village.

Inside the WABAC, Mr. Peabody, Sherman, and Penny looked down at the chaos.

"There's got to be another wormhole somewhere," Mr. Peabody said, determined. Deep in concentration, he scanned the WABAC's display screens. "Aha! There's one!"

He reached across the navigation console and slapped the launch button. Sherman and Penny leaned forward in anticipation. The WABAC's engines surged, propelling them into the wormhole.

Seconds later, the time machine reappeared right where it had started.

Sherman turned to Mr. Peabody. "What happened?" he asked, confused.

"We didn't go anywhere," Penny said uneasily.

Mr. Peabody groaned. "All the wormholes are looping back to the present!" He'd been afraid something like this might happen. "The WABAC has no way back!"

Just then, a police helicopter swooped down in front of the ship. Before Mr. Peabody could react, the chopper launched a giant net. The net fell over the WABAC, putting an end to the time machine's journey. Mr. Peabody had no choice but to land.

The WABAC touched down in the middle of Central Park, which was overrun with historical figures from the time vortex. If Sherman didn't know better, he'd have thought he was looking at a costume party. King Tut and his Egyptian servants raced across the Great Lawn, Robespierre and the French peasants traipsed through Strawberry Fields, and King Agamemnon and his Greek army trooped through Sheep Meadow.

A squadron of police cars arrived with lights flashing and sirens blaring. Miss Grunion jumped out of the lead patrol car, flanked by a troop of police officers.

"Come out, Peabody . . . with your paws in the air!" Miss Grunion ordered.

The door to the WABAC slid open, and Mr. Peabody came out with his paws up. Sherman and Penny followed.

"You're under arrest for kidnapping, reckless endangerment, and a multiplicity of major traffic violations," Miss Grunion informed him.

"You don't understand. If that giant wormhole keeps expanding, it'll rip apart the very fabric of space and time!" Mr. Peabody protested, pointing to the churning vortex in the clouds.

Miss Grunion glowered and clomped over to Mr. Peabody, pushing one finger into his chest. "Blah, blah, blah," she muttered, unimpressed with his excuse. "For too long, you've bamboozled the world with your fancy jargon and that little red tie of yours, and look what's come of it!"

As if on cue, the wind picked up, lightning slashed across the sky, and the Parthenon—a famous Greek temple—dropped out of the vortex. It crashed to the ground just behind the squadron of police cars.

Miss Grunion smirked. The universe had just proved her point. She turned to address the police officers, the historical figures, and the crowd of concerned citizens who had gathered in the park. "This is what happens when you let a DOG adopt a BOY! Take him away!" she shouted, snapping her fingers. "And keep a tighter leash on him this time!"

The policemen hurried forward with a dogcatcher's collar attached to the end of a long pole. Slowly, they closed in. . . .

Mr. Peabody's tail drooped as he watched the police approach. There was nowhere to run and nothing he could do. They snapped the collar around his neck roughly. Mr. Peabody yelped and dropped down on all fours.

"Let me go! You don't know what you're doing!" he yelled. The police ignored him and marched him toward a waiting patrol car like a common dog.

Sherman couldn't bear to see his father treated that way. "What's going to happen to Mr. Peabody?" he asked anxiously.

Miss Grunion fixed him with a dark look. "Don't you know what happens to dogs that bite?" she said threateningly.

Sherman's eyes widened as he realized what Miss Grunion meant. They were going to take Mr. Peabody to the city pound! He couldn't let that happen.

"Wait!" Sherman shouted. "Mr. Peabody is the only one who can fix this problem!"

"Mr. Peabody *is* the problem!" Miss Grunion snarled. "He has systematically broken all the rules!"

"Sure, he has," Sherman said, "but isn't that what all geniuses do? What if Einstein had stopped at E equals mc, with no square? What if Galileo had just said, 'Oh yeah, the sun goes around the Earth, that totally makes sense!'? What if the guy who invented penicillin just threw away the moldy bread? Where would we be then?"

The police stopped in their tracks to consider what Sherman was saying. They looked uncertainly at the talking dog wearing the red bow tie.

Miss Grunion noticed the police officers' hesitation and stomped her foot angrily. "He's through with chances. Now he has to pay for his mistakes!"

Sherman hung his head. He was the one who had made all the mistakes, not Mr. Peabody. "I'm the one who used the WABAC without permission," he confessed. "The only mistake Mr. Peabody ever made . . . was me."

"Sherman?" Mr. Peabody said quietly, his eyes filled with concern.

Miss Grunion whipped her head around and fixed

Sherman with a hard stare. "You're absolutely right, Sherman!" she told him smugly. "A DOG should never have been allowed to adopt a BOY in the first place!"

Sherman knew Miss Grunion thought Mr. Peabody was a bad parent—mostly because he was a dog. But suddenly, he realized that the most important thing Mr. Peabody had taught him was that there was nothing wrong with being a dog—especially a dog like Mr. Peabody.

Sherman's eyes lit up as the truth dawned on him—and with it, a way to save his dad. He squared his shoulders and looked Miss Grunion in the eye. "Maybe you're right, Miss Grunion, but there's one thing you haven't considered," he said.

"What's that?" she asked skeptically. She knew there was nothing this boy could say that would change her mind.

"I'm a dog, too," Sherman answered proudly.

"What?" Miss Grunion said, annoyed.

"If being a dog means you're like Mr. Peabody, who never turns his back on you, and who's always there to pick you up when you fall and loves you no matter how many times you mess up, then yeah, **I'M A DOG, TOO!** Sherman declared.

Mr. Peabody was so proud of Sherman, he could've

howled in delight—but he wasn't really a howler. Instead, he nodded to his boy with a great deal of fatherly affection.

"I'm a dog, too!" yelled Leonardo da Vinci.

"I'm a dog, too!" King Agamemnon shouted.

"I'm a dog, too!" cried Robespierre. "A French poodle."

Sherman's declaration started a chain reaction. One by one, figures from the past and the present came forward to declare themselves dogs. Even Paul Peterson, who'd gotten off to a very rocky start with Mr. Peabody said, "Ditto on that dog thing!"

Last but not least, Penny stepped forward. She'd teased Sherman about being a dog, but now he made her proud to be one. "I'm a dog, too," she said. Penny took Sherman's hand and squeezed it gently.

Sherman blushed and swallowed hard before looking expectantly at Miss Grunion.

Even though he'd won the crowd over, Miss Grunion remained unmoved by Sherman's stirring speech. "All right, fine, you're all dogs, but you can't change the law," she said menacingly.

"*He* can!" Penny said, pointing at a figure in the crowd. It was George Washington, the first president of the United States. He bowed deeply and made his way through the crowd to Mr. Peabody.

22

George Washington cleared his throat. "We hold these truths to be self-evident: that all men—and some dogs—are created equal," the president proclaimed. "I hereby award Mr. Peabody a presidential pardon."

The crowd cheered. The French peasants waved their torches in delight. The Greeks and Trojans beat their swords against their shields. Even King Tut's Egyptian servants set down his royal litter to applaud.

The police released Sherman's father from the dogcatcher's collar. As his first act of freedom, he ran straight to Sherman and gave him a huge hug.

Miss Grunion's frown deepened and her eyes narrowed with rage. "But this is a travesty of justice! He bit me! He should be put down!" she yelled.

Suddenly, a strange whistling noise came from the sky. The time vortex shuddered and spat out a giant Egyptian sphinx. The enormous stone statue with the head of a human and the body of a lion landed with a crash at the opposite end of Central Park.

Everyone turned to look up at the wormhole—Miss Grunion included. It had grown even larger in the past few minutes. Now it took up nearly half the sky. Lightning crackled ominously from its depths.

All the historical figures standing around gathered close to Mr. Peabody.

"Ve have to go home!" said Sigmund Freud in his thick Austrian accent.

"Oui," Marie Antoinette agreed.

"Oui," Robespierre added.

"Dat's vhat I said, ve have to go home!" Freud said insistently.

Mr. Peabody interrupted the three of them and their dueling accents to prevent further misunderstanding. "Unfortunately, it's not going to be that easy. We can't go back to the past," he explained. "But we do have some of the greatest intellects ever assembled. Surely we can work together and come up with a solution!"

Leonardo da Vinci was the first to step forward with an idea. "Why don't we build a giant catapult and fling everyone home?"

Freud didn't like that idea. It might have had something to do with his unconscious fear of flying. He brushed Leonardo's idea aside and asked what kind of relationship the wormhole had with its mother.

Mr. Peabody grimaced. So far, the geniuses were striking out in terms of plans to save the universe.

"Oooh, oooh!" Agamemnon raised his hand excitedly. "I've got an idea! We build a horse and hide inside!"

The French flat-out booed that suggestion, and the historical figures all fell to talking at once.

In the middle of the chaos, Sherman looked up at the time vortex. There had to be a way to set things right. He thought about all the trips he'd taken in the WABAC over the years. He'd traveled to the past and he'd traveled to the present, but he'd never traveled to the future. Sherman's eyes lit up. He had an idea!

"We can't go back to the past, but what about the future?" he said.

"What's that, Sherman?" Mr. Peabody asked. The historical figures fell silent.

"Why not go to the future?" Sherman suggested.

"I've never been there before, so it's probably not as messed up!"

Mr. Peabody turned the idea over in his head. "How would that work, Sherman?"

"If we fly into the future, it'll create a gravitational pull, which will turn the wormhole inside out and send everyone home," Sherman explained.

"Sherman, you're a genius!" Mr. Peabody said, racing toward the WABAC.

Sherman beamed. He dashed after Mr. Peabody but couldn't resist glancing over his shoulder at Penny. "You hear that, Penny? I'm a"—Sherman tripped and stumbled—"genius!"

Penny smirked and waved at Sherman as he stumbled toward the future.

23

Moments later, Mr. Peabody and Sherman climbed on board the WABAC and sat in front of the controls. Sherman watched as his dad punched buttons, flipped levers, and made adjustments to the navigation system.

"So, how far into the future are we gonna go, Mr. Peabody?" Sherman asked eagerly.

"One. Whole. Day," Mr. Peabody answered.

"That doesn't sound very far," Sherman said.

"Far enough to fix the problem," Mr. Peabody replied with a smile. He knew a lot could change in a day. "Would you like to drive, Sherman?"

"Woo-hoo! Yeah!" Sherman nodded enthusiastically. He turned to the controls and activated the time machine's power cells.

The WABAC's engines kicked on.

The whole ship began to vibrate.

"What do you think the future's gonna be like, Mr. Peabody?" Sherman asked.

Mr. Peabody shrugged. "No one has the answer to that question, Sherman."

"Not even you?"

"Not even me."

Sherman pondered for a moment. He looked up at his dad. "Then I guess we'll see it together."

Mr. Peabody smiled, fiercely proud of his son. "I love you, Sherman," he said, his voice full of emotion.

Sherman grinned. "I have a deep and abiding regard for you as well, Mr. Peabody."

Mr. Peabody—scientist, inventor, explorer, Nobel Prize winner, and Olympic gold medalist—opened his arms wide and pulled his son, Sherman, into a hug. He might have studied all the theories of child development, but there was nothing that could have prepared him for the overwhelming love he felt for his son.

He should have known. After all, it didn't take a genius to figure that out, just an average dad.

Sherman leaned forward and punched the glowing red launch button. The WABAC rocketed into the sky and flew straight into the time vortex. There was a giant flash of light, and then suddenly, the wormhole began to close, sucking the historical figures in one by one.

"Auf Wiedersehen!" called Freud.

"Arrivederci!" shouted Leonardo da Vinci.

"Zut alors!" cried Robespierre, which didn't mean goodbye, but it was close enough.

Miss Grunion watched it all from the middle of the park. She was still mad at Mr. Peabody, even though he was saving the world. "You haven't seen the last of me, Peabody!" she shouted, shaking an angry fist. "You'll make a mistake eventually, and when you do, I'll be there!"

The wind picked up as the final historical figure was swept toward the wormhole. It was Agamemnon, and at the last possible moment, he snaked an arm around Miss Grunion. "I've captured the Grunion!" he yelled triumphantly.

It was the last thing anyone heard before the wormhole swallowed them up.

Epilogue

And that, dear reader, is the end of the story. But if you are wondering what happened, Sherman's idea worked wonderfully. Taking the WABAC into the future caused the space-time continuum to snap back into place like a giant rubber band, and the world was saved.

We returned to the dinner party before any of this happened, and I snapped the Petersons out of their trance. The party went on to be a roaring success.

Penny and Sherman became best friends, and she accompanied us on many adventures in the WABAC. But you'll have to read about those some other time.

Yours truly,
Mr. Peabody